# JACK BOYZ N DA BRONX 3

Romell Tukes

Lock Down Publications and
Ca$h
Presents
# Jack Boyz N Da Bronx 3
A Novel by *Romell Tukes*

Romell Tukes

# Lock Down Publications
P.O. Box 944
Stockbridge, Ga 30281
www.lockdownpublications.com

Copyright 2021 by Romell Tukes
Jack Boyz N Da Bronx 3

**Lock Down Publications**
**Like our page on Facebook: Lock Down Publications @**
**www.facebook.com/lockdownpublications.ldp**

Book interior design by:  **Shawn Walker**
Edited by:  **Tamira Butler**

# Stay Connected with Us!

Text **LOCKDOWN** to 22828 to stay up-to-date with new releases, sneak peaks, contests and more...

Thank you!

# Submission Guideline.

Submit the first three chapters of your completed manuscript to ldpsubmissions@gmail.com, subject line: Your book's title. The manuscript must be in a .doc file and sent as an attachment. Document should be in Times New Roman, double spaced and in size 12 font. Also, provide your synopsis and full contact information. If sending multiple submissions, they must each be in a separate email.

Have a story but no way to send it electronically? You can still submit to LDP/Ca$h Presents. Send in the first three chapters, written or typed, of your completed manuscript to:

LDP: Submissions Dept
P.O. Box 944
Stockbridge, Ga 30281

*DO NOT send original manuscript. Must be a duplicate.*

Provide your synopsis and a cover letter containing your full contact information.

Thanks for considering LDP and Ca$h Presents.

# Acknowledgements

First and foremost, I would like to give all praises to Allah. Much love to all the loyal readers rocking with me. Yeah, I know the vibes. Shout out to my family and friends, which are very few. Shout out to Yonkers, New York, we in the building. Shout out Moreno, Spice from Newburgh, OG chuck from BK, my guy Tails from Crown Heights, Dru from the BX-Burnside, shout out Star Brim, Melly from the BX, Nate from Atlanta. Loyalty comes from trust. But it be the ones you say you love the most that will hurt you the worst. Big shout out to Cash the LDP. The game is ours.

Romell Tukes

# Prologue

Michelle Projects BX
Days Prior

Lil' K texted Red, telling her to hurry up so they could go to Blu's funeral.

He wore a black tuxedo for Blu's funeral. Today made him realize family and friends had more value than money and diamonds.

The sky was out and beautiful. The energy in the city was bright. But when he felt a gun to his head, he wished he would have rolled up the window.

Lil' K saw the man's face on his car door mirror and he never saw the mad face until now.

"Revenge is the sweetest thing next to pussy. You first and your brothers next. There's a new cowboy in town," the gunman said.

"Every dog has his day," Lil' K said before the gunman shot him in his head before running off ok. Red saw the text from Lil' K when she was leaving her mom's crib from dropping off money. Red couldn't believe Blu was gone because the whole crew, him and Lil' K, always had her back, even against Banger.

Waiting on the elevator, she heard a loud gunshot, which made her reach for her gun, and rushed outside.

When she made it outside, she saw nobody, then she went to the car to ask Lil' K what happened.

"Noooooooo!" Red screamed at the top of her lungs when seeing a small gunshot wound to his head.

Red felt for a pulse and luckily, he had one, which meant he was alive. She was sent to the nearest hospital.

An hour later, the doctor came out and told her Lil' K was going to make it, so the bullet missed his brain.

Red left the hospital to call Kazzy Loc and Knight to tell him what happened. She got in touch with Knight then she called Kazzy Loc.

While on the phone with Kazzy, she was ambushed and kidnapped.

\*\*\*

Meanwhile, Across Town

Kazzy Loc heard everything that went on while on the phone with Red. He was rushing to leave his crib, calling Knight, and when he opened the door, men were there with their weapons drawn.

The gunmen took Kazzy Loc with them.

Knight was listening to everything going on, and he knew something big was going down. As he was driving, a big truck parked in front of Knight and a man jumped out shooting, but Knight crawled out of his car, firing back at the man.

A man ended up hitting Knight from behind, taking him down. Once he was on the floor, the goons took him down, placing a pillowcase over his head.

\*\*\*

Washington Heights New York

Paco was trying to call everybody, but nobody was picking up. He needed more bricks. He had Washington Heights on a lot with his crew moving weight.

He went into one of his apartment buildings, where he kept his stash, to see his goons.

Inside the crib, he saw both of his workers dead on the living room floor, but the drugs and money were still there.

Not wanting to be around when the police came, he left, waiting on the elevator.

When the elevator doors opened, gunmen attacked Paco, taking him to the floor and placing zip ties on his wrists and ankles, carrying him off.

Romell Tukes

# Chapter 1

Harare, Zimbabwe

Knight, Kazzy Loc, Red, and Paco all were seated in chairs with pillow cases over their heads with breathing holes in them.

There was some type of large underground room full of African men with high-powered assault rifles and swords. A dark-skinned older man walked into the room with a salt and pepper beard.

"Take off their coverings, now!" he shouted with his deep voice.

His men did as they were told in a hurry while the older man stood in front of the group.

The man was Khalid. He was the biggest drug supplier in Zimbabwe, where he grew heroin in his farms. He had strong ties all over the world. His kids were all trained killers, except two raised in the states. Khalid had four wives whom he loved to death and treated all equally. He loved his Muslim religion, but he also loved the life of sin.

"Undo the tape from around their mouths, you fucking dummies!" Khalid shouted in his African accent.

"Yo, what the fuck?" Kazzy Loc said, pissed, looking around, wondering where they were at.

Kazzy remembered them being on a plane, but had no clue where they were now.

"Who are you?" Paco asked the question all four of them were thinking.

"You gentlemen robbed one of my workers," Khalid stated.

"We robbed a lot of people, champ. You gotta take that loss. It's all a part of the game," Knight told him.

"Knight, I thought outta everybody in your crew, you would be the smarter one," Khalid said.

"Maybe you think too much," Knight shot back.

"Y'all robbed Saint, my wife's son, but I'll let that slide because that's not y'all fault. The person who gave Saint up will pay the price," Khalid said as Red thought about Bugatti, who put them on to the Saint lick.

"So, what the fuck do you want? If you're gonna kill us, just do it, because you're killing the vibe," Red said.

"A little lady with a vicious mouth. My son was right about you, but I'm not here to kill y'all, it's the opposite," Khalid stated.

"You lost me, fam, because the way you came for us, I couldn't tell if you wanted us killed or murdered," Knight said.

"There is no difference." Khalid looked confused

"My point made." Knight made Paco laugh.

"Maybe our mutual friend can explain to you Americans better than I can. Son, come out!" Khalid shouted.

When everybody saw Bugatti Boy come through the doors, their faces dropped, especially Red. She felt betrayed.

"I know what you all are thinking, but y'all in good hands. There is another life to me that y'all ain't know about, because I just found out myself. This is my dad, and he wants to give us a chance of a lifetime to take over the drug trade."

"We will become rich," Bugatti Boy told them. "Uncuff them, y'all niggas bugging out," Bugatti Boy stated, upset.

The men uncuffed everybody.

"We have our plug," Knight stated.

"Stephen is a chomp change to us. You have to take risks in the game, as you know," Khalid said.

"What if we don't want your offer?" Paco asked.

"Then so be it, but it's something to sleep on. Y'all can enjoy Africa. You all have your own master bedrooms. Bugatti will show you around, but please, join me for dinner," Khalid said before walking off with his goons.

Red got up and slapped Bugatti Boy so hard he felt blood in his mouth.

"You betrayed us. You corny for that, my nigga. Lil' K laying in the hospital, Blu funeral passed, and you got us out here in Africa looking stupid," she said with tears because she missed Lil' K.

"I'm sorry." Bugatti Boy knew she was right, so he didn't argue with her.

"Show us around. I need a shower," Kazzy Loc said as everybody else agreed.

Romell Tukes

# Chapter 2

Zimbabwe

Bugatti Boy looked at himself in a big mirror hanging on his wall, and his master bedroom looked like an apartment.

He couldn't believe what was taking place. If he would have been on his father's status, he could have been rich and put his crew on instead of running the streets doing crazy shit.

When his father's goons kidnapped him, he tried to run, until they tased him and tackled him.

They did him the same way they did his team. When he met Khalid and heard him explain everything, he hated his mother for not telling him about Khalid.

His mom told him his father was in prison once, then she told him his dad got killed. Whenever he asked about his dad, she would say her husband was his dad, but he and his sister knew better, even though they called him dad.

Bugatti Boy wished he could have been there when his boy Lil' K got shot. He couldn't believe it, but Red felt it the worst because of how close they were. Blu's death had been on his mind heavy. He wanted payback whenever he got back to the states.

His father already knew about Knight and the crew. Khalid felt like they could be a big help to his drug enterprise in the states.

Bugatti never knew he had more sisters until his father recently introduced him to Bahadi and Nasma. Both women were very beautiful and killers.

He left his room and made his way to Red's room. He saw the look on her face, and he knew she was pissed at him.

Never would he betray his friends. He felt like this was a chance of a lifetime for them all.

Red took a shower and got dressed in a nice designer dress that she saw laid out on the bed for her.

She didn't want to be in Africa right now playing games with some African prince wanna be.

Red needed to be with her man and looking for the person or crew responsible for the attempt on Lil' K's life.

"Red, can I come in?" a voice said from the other side of the door. She was fully dressed already but didn't feel like talking to anybody at the moment.

"Bugatti, get the fuck away from my door!" she shouted.

"Red, hear me out on the set. It's not what you think." Bugatti Boy knew why she was upset, but he needed her to see things the way he did for the future.

"You have 60 seconds," she stated, then he came in the room looking crazy as she gave him an evil look.

"I know you're mad, but Lil' K is good, and we will find his shooter. This is big, Red. We don't gotta rob or kill no more. This is our big break."

"Well, that is not about the money, drug, or a plug, it's about family and loyalty!" she yelled loudly, getting mad.

"I know, Red, that's why we are all here, so we can build a bigger family. We are about to be international," he added.

"I know you had nothing but good intentions, Bugatti, but you don't even know these niggas."

Bugatti knew she made a firm point, so he didn't even argue back with her. He took it for what it was worth.

"Are you with me?" Bugatti asked before he stepped out the door.

"I'm always with you, Bugatti Boy, but stop being so dumb." She made him laugh as he walked out to be prepared for dinner.

\*\*\*

Everybody sat in the dining room around a big table full of all types of meat and food.

"I'm glad you all could make it. Once again, I apologize for the kidnapping, but I know all of your resumes, so I had to be cautious," Khalid stated, sitting at the head of table.

"Where is my little brother at?" Knight asked the question that was on everybody's mind.

"He's on a private flight here, and the private jet should land on my private runway in the back, if you are agreeable to my offer."

Red picked up the fork off the table, but Kazzy held her hand, already knowing what she wanted to do.

"Now you are playing dangerous games," Bugatti Boy spoke up.

"Son, this is business, not personal. I would like for you all to expand my heroin product and coke. I'm charging you barely nothing. I will send you tons monthly to market all over New York, knocking your competition out the water," Khalid stated.

"You're willing to do all of this by force, which makes me believe you have other hidden agendas," Kazzy spoke up as Paco nodded his head.

"Big words, but I can see why you would consider that, Kazzy. I'm a businessman who gets everything he wants, whether I ask nicely or have to take it. Y'all know how the game goes." Khalid's maid brought out trays of fruit, which was normal in Africa to welcome guests.

"We have a deal, but let us make sure Lil' K is good before we come into agreement," Knight said.

They all knew Knight was about to sell all their souls to the devil.

"I must let you all know now we have a big family. I had opponents we may have to crush." Khalid saw no fear in any of their eyes, which made him feel comfortable with his choice.

"We don't care about that. We want to make sure Lil' K is ok first," Red said.

"Do we have a deal?" Khalid asked.

"Yes, I told you we do," Knight added.

"Okay, bring him out!" Khalid yelled.

Seconds later, two big African men carried out a man with a pillowcase over his head as he was trying to get loose.

The guard set the man in the chair as everybody looked at him.

Khalid got up and took the pillowcase off Lil' K's head.

"Oh my god," Red said, in tears, as she saw a headwrap around his head with a blood stain.

"You dirty nigger," Kazzy told Khalid.

Khalid took the duct tape from over Lil' K's mouth and came out as he looked around.

"Y'all good?" Lil' K looked around, wondering what was going on.

"We'll fill you in later. This is our new plug. He kidnapped us all so we can work for him." Knight kept it short.

"Red, you're good, baby?" Lil' K saw her in tears, then she got up and left the table.

"I had him here for a couple of days. One of my daughters is a nurse and took good care of him and his head shot," Khalid said, looking at Lil' K.

"Since we are family now, when will this business start?" Kazzy asked, being funny, but nobody laughed except Paco, who sat there quiet the whole time.

"Soon. In the meantime, the Motherland, it's beautiful."

"Fuck the motherland. When you ready to talk money, pull up on us. Come on, Lil' K," Knight said, leaving Khalid alone.

# Chapter 3

### Africa

Knight and Lil' K sat in a large room filled with fish tanks and fancy African artwork.

"You got it, bro?" Knight asked his little brother, pouring himself a drink of cognac.

"I'm good, this ain't about shit. I'm glad I made it," Lil' K stated.

"Despite our new current situation with this Khalid nigga, we still got a major issue back home, and it could be useful for us." Knight sat down, trying to make sense of what he just got everybody into.

"You don't think he's going to cause havoc on what we built?" Lil' K didn't trust Khalid at all, and he knew dealing with Khalid would soon cause discord.

"No, because he will always have a disadvantage." Knight saw Lil' K's disarrayed look. "Follow my lead, little bro, we good. I advise you to go holla at Red and get your mind back in the game," Knight stated as Lil' K got up and went to find Red through the biggest mansion he'd ever seen.

Lil' K couldn't get the man who shot him out his head, and the voice. When he woke up in the hospital, he remembered hearing Red's voice as she drove him to the hospital. He walked to her room in deep thought.

"There was a writer named Stendhal who once quoted, 'Glances are the heavy artillery of the flirt. Everything can be conveyed in a look, yet that can always be denied, for it cannot be quoted word for word.'" Lil' K sat down at the end of the bed as Red sat up with red, puffy eyes.

"This isn't the time for games, Lil' K. "Red turned on the lamp, letting him see the indignation on her face.

Lil' K could tell she was in her bag, but she had every reason to be upset.

"Baby, everything happens for a reason, and I sat in the hospital bed thinking about all the shit we could have done better. We lost Blu and Banger, then almost lost me if you ain't save me." Lil' K saw her beautiful, flawless skin, which he loved.

"Shit happens," she said in a sharp tone.

"I know, but this could be a new start for us. We are family now, and we all we got." Lil' K crawled into the bed with her.

"Oh, hell no, nigger, you better get in the shower, you smell." Red pushed him, laughing.

"You coming with me?"

"You know that, daddy." She got out of the bed and went with him to the bathroom.

Red and Lil' K made love on the sink, on the toilet, on the marble floor, and in the glass shower. Red sucked on his dick so good, he almost pulled her hair out, and she caught all his kids, swallowing and everything.

***

Paco took a late-night walk around the compound, and he had some weed to smoke.

The sky was filled with bright stars and a full moon tonight. It looked soothing.

He saw a woman sitting alone in Muslim attire.

"Can I join you?" he asked.

"If you want." The woman's voice wasn't as strong as Khalid's or his maids. Her voice sounded like she lived in America most of her life.

"What's your name?" Paco asked, as the woman gave him an inarticulate look. Paco could not believe how sexy the Muslim woman was.

"Nasma."

"I'm Paco."

"I know who you are, playboy," she shot back.

"It's like that?"

"It's no point of you wasting your breath." She got up with an assault rifle that laid by her side.

"I just needed someone to talk to, please don't go." Paco saw he now had her attention, as her eyes softened up, waiting for this day, but she knew it was against her father Khalid's rules to speak to guests.

"One day, I can't now." Nasma rushed off into a private building with all the guards who lived and trained.

Paco couldn't shake her beauty or her sweet voice. He got up and went to find Bugatti to get the scoop on Nasma.

*** 

## Brooklyn, NY

Money steered his all-white Jaguar through the Brooklyn streets to meet up with his plug and discuss business.

Knight was my cousin. Money's father was Uncle Sam, who Money killed in Virginia years ago.

When his father got murdered, he was locked up in state prison for an attempted murder charge he did 10 years on.

Now at 26 years old, Money wanted to get to the bag. He was from Albany, NY, where he grew up with his mom, step-dad, and sister. Selling drugs in Albany, New York was making him rich, thanks to Fats who found him a while back and told him about Knight killing his dad, Slim.

Money knew he had family in the Bronx, but he never met them because he spent most of his childhood in prison.

He had some status in his blood set. He was a big homie in the street.

Shooting Lil' K in his head did him justice, but he really wanted Knight. He just couldn't get the drop on him.

Money knew Big Blazer and Holiday from prison, so when he heard they had beef with the same crew, he reached out to Holiday.

Money recently got a crib in the Bronx and Brooklyn so he could track down the crew.

# Chapter 4

## Africa

Knight and Kazzy played chess in the living room, which looked like a mini mall.

The chess pieces were made out of crystal glass and hand carved.

"Your move," Knight said, taking Kazzy's bishop.

"I ain't know we were on a timer, fam, and the next piece you touch, you move." Kazzy hated losing in chess.

"Nigger, both of you niggas trash," Paco said, watching the game from a distance.

"What are you, a cheerleader?" Kazzy got frustrated wherever he lost a game.

Knight checkmated him after his last move, winning the game.

"Good game, champ," Knight said to his brother as Lil' K and Red came inside the living room.

"Y'all coming?" Lil' K asked everybody as he and Red walked side by side.

"To where?" Paco asked.

"Training day." Lil' K walked off.

## Thirty Minutes Later

Two vans pulled up to a small forest area leading into the jungle.

"Y'all going hunting." Khalid hopped out a doorless Jeep with four African men.

The African men passed everybody assault rifles with a knife attached to the end of the weapons.

"What type of games are you playing, son?" Knight stated.

"This will be good for you all to use when you go back home," Khalid stated.

"But this is a jungle," Red said, thinking that shit was dumb.

"My point, life is a jungle, so why not learn how to survive in a real jungle around real animals?" Khalid wanted them to see how it felt to hunt and kill real tigers and lions.

"So, what are we about to do?" Paco asked, admiring the assault rifle with the wood-grain handle.

"It's six of y'all, so there will be two groups divided into three. Two of my guards will be with each group, just in case it gets a little extreme," Khalid said before walking off, going back in the Jeep and driving off.

"This nigga tripping." Bugatti Boy couldn't believe he was about to go on a dumb ass mission.

"That's your pops." Knight led the pack through the woods.

A tiger almost killed Bugatti, but Lil' K shot so many rounds in the tiger's stomach he did a 360.

\*\*\*

Bronx, New York

6'7 was a tall, stocky nigger with a bad attitude. They called him 6'7 because of his height. He sold grams of coke in the Patterson projects.

His connect was his brother, Holiday, who worked under Big Blazer in the Soundview area.

"Where Puff at? That nigga owe me a half a pound of loud, son, that's a fact." 6'7 walked up to two young ladies standing on the corner on a late night, waiting for customers.

"Puff Uptown with some thots he met days ago," one of the young niggas said, unaware of the gray Toyota sedan that just pulled up on the block.

6'7 had a lot of beef with niggas from other hoods, so he was always on point. He saw three gunmen hop out the car with guns and go into action.

*Boc...*

*Boc...*

*Boc...*

*Boc...*

*Boc...*

6'7 shot over the two young boys, using one of them as a shield.

He saw one of his young boys go down with two shots to the neck.

*Boc...*

*Boc...*

The bullets from 6'7's gun knocked down another shooter as the last gunman ran.

"We got to bounce, yo." 6'7 grabbed his young boys, running up the block.

\*\*\*

## Webster Avenue, BK
## Weeks Later

Big Blazer rolled around in a white G Wagon SUV with a pistol on his lap.

He recently got back in town from laying low in North Carolina, opening up shop with a crew he met while he was down there.

Since he'd been back in the Bronx, he hadn't heard anything about Knight and his crew, which he found odd.

The town was dead except his hood, Soundview.

His childhood friend, Holiday, had the city on lock with the brick game while he was going on his little vacation. There was only one thing on Big Blazer's mind, and that was to get Knight and his crew.

# Chapter 5

Africa
2 months later…

Lil' K walked into the room to see Red reading a noble Quran.

"What's up baby, how are you doing?" he asked Red as he sat down next to her, smelling her perfume scent.

"Hey, just doing some reading." She closed the Quran and sat it down next to the night lamp.

Lately, she'd been reading into Islam and so had Lil' K. Islam was practiced heavily in Africa and she liked everything about the culture.

"We should be leaving here within a couple of days," Lil' K said.

"I know, but to be honest, I want to take my Shahada." She saw the surprised look on his face.

"I want to also, so I've been thinking about it heavy," Lil K stated seriously.

"When did you plan on telling me?" she asked.

"When did you plan on it?" he shot back.

"I wanted to do it when we went back to New York, but I think Africa, the motherland." Red looked at him in his eyes to see if he was sincere about this.

"You want to have Khalid do it?" Lil' K stated.

"I mean… Why not? He's a devoted Muslim, and I read all you need is three Muslims as a witness."

"You ready?" Lil' K stood up.

"Right now, babe?"

"It's in your heart, right?" Lil' K shot back, ready to become a Muslim. This was the only thing right he felt he'd done in his life.

"Aight." Red followed him downstairs to Khalid's mosque area in the basement.

Khalid and Bugatti Boy were in his mosque, talking with seven African guards standing around on patrol.

"Lil' K and Red, my friends, how's everything?" Khalid asked.

"We want to take a Shahada." Lil' K's voice was stern.

"Both of you?" Khalid asked, somewhat shocked.

"Yeah, nigga, he's going to 21 Questions us, do it." Red wasn't in the mood for games, and she just disliked Khalid.

"Y'all serious?" Bugatti Boy looked at both of them.

"Let's do it then," Khalid said, giving them their shahada as they embraced Islam.

\*\*\*

Harlem New York

6'7 been laying low for the last couple of months after killing his ops.

He only came out at night time from his baby mother's crib on Lenox. She was a cute dark-skin chick who worked at a local shopping center.

His car was parked at the end of the corner next to his baby mother's Honda sedan.

"Excuse me, but are you 6'7?" A pretty, brown, thick chick approached him with nice eyes.

"Facts, ma, who you?" 6'7 eyed her nice curves and fat pussy poking out of her jeans, looking behind him to make sure his hating ass baby mother wasn't in the window watching.

"NYPD, get down on the fucking ground, dumbass." The woman pulled out her work weapon.

6'7 got down on the ground slowly as cops came out from everywhere with guns drawn.

6'7 knew better than to make any funny movement, because cops were killing shit all over New York.

\*\*\*

Minutes Later

"You're being charged with two murders. That's a good seventy years or more in prison, maybe life," a cop said, standing up trying to read 6'7.

"Man, I ain't doing shit! Bitch, suck a dick."

"That's what your mouth says," the detective woman said, sitting down ice grilling. The sexy woman's name was Det. Valentines.

"What y'all want?" 6'7 said the key words as the two homicide cops looked at each other as if they hit the jackpot.

"Tell us who you and your crew work for?" the woman cop asked.

"Will this shit get back to me? Because I got a name to uphold," he said, making a cop on the wall laugh.

"Your name will never be exposed," she said.

"Okay, my brother, Holiday, works for Big Blazer," 6'7 stated

"Can you get them to admit to drug trafficking and murder?" she asked, feeling it was her big break. Her partner bet her $100 she wouldn't break him in an hour.

"Yes, I can."

"Give me my fucking hundred," she told her partner.

Romell Tukes

# Chapter 6

Canon USP Prison, PA

"Get money, blood, get money, blood... up... down... up... down let's go," D Fatal Brim yelled to 14 prisoners exercising in the prison yard.

In the feds, inmates did a lot of burpees and cardio to replace the absence of weights.

D Fatal Brim became a workout machine after being locked up. Now he was training his homies so they stayed war ready.

"Five minutes, blood, turn that shit up," the D Fatal Brim shouted minutes before they shut the yard down.

He had a visit in a couple of hours with a new chick he met on a dating site.

Knight visited recently and sent him a letter, telling him he'd been on vacation in Africa and it was beautiful. Knight told D Fatal Brim that he was at the highlight of his career, and he knew what that meant.

Everybody from the streets was still in tune with him, except Less, who was still locked up in New York State Prison.

The yard cleared and D Fatal Brim went back to his unit to use the Corrlinks email and phone.

\*\*\*

Fishkill New York

Head drove up to Fishkill Prison where his boy, Baggs, just got released after a five-year bid.

Lil' Baby's new album played in his car as he sang the words, feeling the Atlanta rapper's lyrics.

Head put on for the Soundview and Castle Hill section of the Bronx. He was Holiday's cousin, but the two moved differently in the streets.

Holiday was the flashy, loud type, and Head liked to be relaxed and outta sight unless it was war time.

Being 29 years old, raised in the streets, Head learned a lot. His dad was a retired kingpin who ran a small plumbing business with Head's younger brother.

Pulling up to the front of the jail's tailgates, he saw Baggs walking out with a small bag in his hand.

Baggs felt like a new man walking out of prison.

The last five years, Baggs had been to four prisons. He started off in a maximum-security prison then went on his way down to a medium-level security spot. Five years ago, he got convicted of first-degree robbery with a gun in his hood, Soundview.

Now, at 30 years old, Baggs had one thing on his mind, and that was getting to a bag. While being in jail, the only names he was hearing about in there were Glock and Big Blazer.

When Big Blazer and Holiday used to send him pictures, he used to show the whole unit his homies in Rolls Royces, jewelry, designer clothes, and with money.

Baggs and Head were both a part of the SMM crew under Big Blazer.

"Yoooo…" Baggs yelled as he approached Head.

"What's the vibes?" Heads shot back, seeing how big his boy got lifting them weights.

"You know the vibes. Let's slide before I got to slap one of these bum ass officers and walk past them into the jail."

"We out, son. I got you an Adidas tracksuit in the back with a pair of Jordan's," Head said, driving down the hill leading to the main street.

"Where Big Blazer and Holiday? I thought they were pulling up, fam."

"Nah they had to handle some real serious business out of town," Head stated.

"Aight, what's going on in the hood?" Baggs asked, missing Soundview projects.

"Shit different, bro, it's all bad. Niggas getting killed, bitches who we went to school with are selling pussy and smoking base," Head said.

"Damn, bro." Baggs listened to Lil' Baby and closed his eyes.

\*\*\*

Bronx New York

Knight and the whole crew all waited in an abandoned factory in Hunts Points for Bugatti Boy to pull up with the first shipment sent by Khalid.

"Yoo, son, what if the shit is trash?" Paco asked Kazzy, who gave him an annoyed look.

"Nigga, you talk too much," Red said, as headlights approached them.

Bugatti Boy parked the commercial U-Haul van inside the factory as everybody surrounded it.

"We lit, y'all, but who drives this shit around the Bronx? I'm not. I was odee scared, picking this shit out," Bugatti Boy said, opening the back doors to show them rolls of bricks stacked halfway to the roof.

"God damn," Lil' K said, seeing tons of keyz.

"Call the guys and tell them to come pick this shit up," Knight told Kazzy.

Less than 30 minutes later, trucks pulled up, loading up all the drugs in four different SUVs.

Romell Tukes

# Chapter 7

Queens, New York

The arena was filling up in and out as people parked their cars in the large parking lot.

Summer Jam took place every year in the city, and everybody came out to watch the hottest rappers and singers perform. Tory Lanez, Callboy, Quavo, and Lil' Durk came out today to shut it down.

Holiday pulled up into the parking lot in a new red BMW I8 with the doors in the air, blasting Meek Mill's old song, "I'm A Boss."

Three cars trailed him. One car was full of his sister's girlfriends and the others with his goons. Holiday rolled deep whenever he went, especially big events.

His sister, Avona, sat next to him in the passenger seat, looking like a doll. She had golden skin, long curly hair, big titties, and a big ass with no stomach since she got her body done. Her chinky eyes and cute face got her a lot of attention since her youth.

"I am on the lower level. Meet me back here. Don't be running off, acting fresh," he texted her as he parked.

"Boy, bye, I'm twenty-one years old, not five." Avona got into his car with rips in her jeans, showing her ass cheeks.

"Thot," he mumbled under his breath, as she got out and got up with four of her girls who came with her. Holiday paid for all of their tickets.

A group of goons walked with him inside the place to see close to a million people everywhere. The place was turned up. Niggas were drinking and smoking in the crowds. Everybody had guns on them since there was no search or metal detectors at the gate.

Holiday saw a nice looking woman in a designer outfit with Jimmy Choo heels, looking sexy, showing her manicured toes. She had nice, slim curves, but her face caught his attention.

"What's the vybeez, ma?" Holiday approached the woman in front of her friends.

"You tell me," the woman replied, sipping on a Nutcracker liquor drink.

"You're sexy, and I'm trying to build with you," Holiday yelled over the loud music.

"How about you just take my number and hit me when the shit over," she shot back, giving him her number.

"What's your name?" he asked.

"BeBe, what's yours?"

"Howard, but keep that on the law, you heard, ma." Holiday gave her his full name.

"I will." He and BeBe kicked it until the show was almost over and it got dark.

Avona and her friends left early out of the arena to chill in the parking lot where it was litty at.

"You see that nigga eyeing you girl, sitting on the green Porsche?" one of Avona's friends pointed out to her, walking through crowds of people.

"That nigga ain't looking at me, bitch." Avona looked at some cute, fly ass Spanish nigga blowing smoke out his mouth, watching her.

"Gurl you better go holler at that fine ass nigga before I do, big factz," her fat friend stated, joking, but she was also serious.

"Y'all holler if y'all see Holiday and his servants." Avona walked up to the man looking at her.

"Excuse me, but my friends think you were watching me, is that true?" She didn't know what to say, but she hopped she ain't sound dumb.

"I admire beauty, and you definitely epitomize it. That's why I couldn't take my eyes off of you." Paco smiled at her.

Avona's heart started to race. She'd never felt like this.

"Well, I'm about to leave, so how about we exchange numbers and get up another day?" she said, pulling her iPhone out of her bag.

"I don't think that's a good idea," Paco told her, seeing a disappointed look on her face.

"Why, I'm not good enough?"

"It's not that, you're perfect me. I just live a different type of lifestyle," he said.

"I don't care. I want to get to know you," she demanded.

"Ok." He took her phone, put his number in it, and got in his car, leaving her there.

Paco only came out to see who was out shining and stunting so he could make them a lick soon. Even though his team had enough keys to flood New York State, he still had the hunger for jacking drug dealers.

He realized in the parking lot that she had to be the tenth chick to pull up on him tonight.

Paco was able to get six license plate numbers of some big ballers, and he planned to have his boy look into the DMV so he can get their addresses.

Romell Tukes

# Chapter 8

Brooklyn, New York

Money got off the downtown exit to meet up with Fat, his plug. Things for him and his crew were sweet since dealing with Fats.

His main focus at the moment was finding Knight and his crew, because word in the street was Knight was back.

Money knew Lil' K and Knight were brothers, so he knew Knight would feel some type of way when he found out who killed his brother. What didn't make sense to Money about the whole thing had to be Lil' K not having a funeral.

He pulled into the garage parking lot.

Every day he thought about the death of his dad, Slim, and how Knight, his own family, killed him. Even though his dad was not in his life growing up, he still considered him his dad. Money heard the rumors of his dad working with the feds to get out of jail, but he didn't fully believe it.

He took the stairs to Fats' condo on the top floor.

Fats watched *The Martin Show* on the BET Network, something he did almost every morning.

Being one of the biggest kingpins in New York, Fats loved every second of the fame. He wanted to be the only kingpin in New York City, but he knew that would only be a dream.

Fats reached out to Money a while back, shedding light on who killed his pops. Since kids, Fats learned how to master other people's minds, and he used people until there was no more left in them.

He needed Money to muscle Knight and his crew out of the Bronx, so he could take over. Everything was a business to him.

When Glock was alive, he used him as his muscle, but things went left and he ended up dying. His next victim, Big Blazer, tried, but his time was cut short when he moved down south, but he was now back.

With Big Blazer, Money, and Fats' son, Lil' Mike, on his team, New York belonged to him. The doorbell rang and he knew Money was supposed to pull up.

"What's goodie?" Fats turned on his young nigga swag.

"Ain't shit, bro." Money walked into the condo to smell a cherry scent in the air.

The luxurious condo had glass stairs, a private master wing, a massive stone fireplace in the living room, a beam ceiling, and a chef's dream kitchen.

"I'm glad you came. Lil' Mike asked about you last night when we went out," Fats stated, sitting down in the living room.

"He still in the Bronx?"

"Yeah, back and forth, setting up shop from Brooklyn to the Bronx."

"Aight, what's the word?"

"I got some bad news for you, fam. I just found out." Fats hated to be the one to crush dreams, especially when Money felt like he was up.

"What?"

"Lil' K survived the shooting," said Fats, as a surprised look enveloped Money's face.

"Damn, yo…"

"You'll get him next time, but they're back in town, so you know what time it is." Fat knew Money was disappointed, but he knew he would go extra hard next time.

\*\*\*

Miami Florida

Knight and Kazzy were in Miami in a rental, on their way to meet with Stephen at a beach.

"What do you think she's going to say when you tell her you found a new plug?" Kazzy asked, looking at the beautiful city of beautiful women and palm trees.

"I don't know, but we were kinda put in a tight spot. I'm sure she'll try to understand," Knight said, pulling into the lot of a beach.

"If she starts tripping, I'ma plug her ass up." Kazzy pulled out his gun he got from one of his crips from Carol City.

"It's no need for that. Me and Stephen got history, bro," Knight got out.

"I knew you hit that." Kazzy knew there was something more than business when it came to them.

"I ain't say that, bro, so get that outta your head, shawty official." Knight saw Stephen laying alone on a towel on the beach, watching people who were still coming out.

"Oh my god, Knight," Stephen yelled, jumping up in her bikini, running into Knight's arm with her ass and titties out.

Kazzy just stood there looking at her body.

"You look nice." Knight checked her out.

"I try… What's up, Kazzy?" She looked at Kazzy.

"Hey," Kazzy said flatly.

"Can we talk?" Knight asked.

"Sure, let's walk." Stephen grabbed his hand and they walked the beach as if they were a couple. StephenStephen always moved as if there were eyes on her. She was always on point.

"I was kidnapped by some African niggars." Knight felt sand fill up his Louis Vuitton loafers.

"Khalid?" she asked with a menacing tone.

"How you know?"

"He is bad business, Knight, and he hates me, so he would do anything to destroy what I have. Khalid made you a target and blackmailed you?"

"Yeah, but cool, I'm coming up with something." Knight saw something in her eyes.

"It's not that easy, Knight. Once Khalid has you by the neck, you're his forever. Trust me, you're not the first client of mine he did this to."

"I know what I'm doing, ma. I just wanted to tell you what's going on. Until I fix this, I need to be excused from business," he said.

"Okay, thanks." Stephen walked off, leaving Knight looking into the ocean.

# Chapter 9

### East Burnside, BX

Lil' Milk had the drug flow on Burnside doing numbers since he opened up shop with his boy Dee.

Lil' Mike knew how to hustle at the young age of nineteen. Fats tossed him keyz for free because he was his son, but Lil' Mike didn't want anything for free.

Growing up, Fats was never there for him to raise him like most kids growing up nowadays.

When he met his dad years ago, Lil' Mike showed no type of emotion till this day. Lil' Mike looked at Fats as a brother or plug rather than a father.

Fats had so many kids, Lil' Mike didn't even know who his brothers or sisters were. Every month a new woman his dad used to fuck with in the past was claiming he got her pregnant.

"How we looking today, fam?" Lil' Mike walked into the corner store.

"Yep," the man behind the counter said, handing him a brown paper bag full of money.

"Aight, say less, son, I will be back later with two keys," Lil' Mike said before walking out the store.

***

### Soundview, BX

The warm day put Holiday in a good mood as he drove to surprise 6'7 for his birthday.

His brother had been acting funny and he wanted to see what was going on with him, because this wasn't like him at all.

Pulling up to a Six-Seven's side bitch's crib, he saw six-seven getting out of a black detective's car down the block.

Holiday turned off his car engine and leaned back behind his tints, looking at the cop car roll by to see two cops inside.

"What the fuck?" Holiday had been in the game for a long time, and he knew when a nigga was about to give it up and violate the G-Code.

Before pulling off, he saw his phone light up and it was six-seven blowing his phone up.

"Yo," Holiday answered his phone.

"What's up, bro?"

"Cooling, how are you?" Holiday stated, nonchalant.

"I need forty keys of coke, bro. Can you drop it off to me tonight?" Six-Seven asked bluntly.

"Damn, bro, it's your birthday. You forgot, son?" Holiday stated.

"Oh, yeah, good looks. I was so busy," Six-Seven shot back.

"Where are you at?" Holiday asked.

"I'm in Long Island, but I'll be back at 10 p.m. to meet you for them forty keys of coke."

"I have no clue what you're talking about, but take care bro," Holiday said before hanging up on his brother.

Six-Seven never talked crazy on the phone or lied about his location, so he knew it was a set up.

\*\*\*

Fordham, BX

Red picked up some clothes and sneakers for Lil' K just to do something nice for him.

She liked doing shopping at night time, because it was peaceful and less people were out, but tonight Fordham was packed with shoppers.

Since being back in New York, it felt like she didn't miss out on a thing.She and Lil' Kgot a new crib in a nice area away from the hood.

Red had focused on rebuilding with Lil' K and learning their Islamic being. She reached out to her old getting money crew to let them know it was time to paper chase again, and they were ready.

Red was walking down the block with a handful of bags from Jimmy Jazz clothing store. Her car was parked on the side block surrounded by buildings and alleys. She saw big rats running around the sidewalks and streets freely.

She popped the trunk to her car to toss the bags inside.

"Bitch, I dare you to move. I'll blow your shit off, ya heard me?" the voice said from behind her.

"Slow down, you got the wrong bitch," Red said, not moving.

"I heard y'all was back, so I'm making you the first vic," he told her.

Head had been on her since he saw she left out of Foot Locker where his little sister worked. He was surprised she didn't see him.

A man on a motorcycle roared toward him with a gun aimed in his direction.

*Boc...*

*Boc...*

*Boc...*

Head didn't move fast enough and caught a bullet to the shoulder. Red pulled out a gun from her purse and was already up the street.

"Fuck, bitch ass nigga," Red yelled.

Bugatti Boy got off the bike.

"You good, Red?"

"Yeah, we got to go before the cops get here. Call me later," she said, getting inside her car.

# Chapter 10

Soho, New York

Knight met with a rich white guy and they discussed the business of opening a new club together. A few hours later, Knight went out to eat alone in a nice button-up shirt and slacks. The atmosphere in the restaurant was peaceful and sublime.

"Can I help you with anything?" A cute waiter approached the table.

"Yes, can you order that beautiful woman sitting near the window your finest bottle of wine?" Knight asked, looking at the brown-skin woman he couldn't keep his eyes off of.

"Okay, no problem." She walked off, a little jealous.

Later that night, Knight had a meeting with the crew because Big Blazer and his homies were in the Bronx, out for blood.

Knight knew once you beef with a nigga, the beef wasn't over until someone laid six-feet deep, especially when blood was drawn.

The waitress brought the bottle over to the woman and Knight saw her look at him and tell the waitress no thank you.

Knight saw the waitress walk off with the bottle of wine, so he figured the woman didn't drink it, and he felt dumb.

Thinking of a plan B, he got up and made his way over to the woman's table, a little nervous for some reason.

"Hey, I'm sorry to interrupt, but I hope I didn't offend you with the wine. I just saw you sitting over here alone, so I thought it's the right thing to do," Knight stated, seeing her give off a little blush.

"Thanks, I appreciate that, but I don't drink," she said.

"Can I have a seat, if you don't mind?" he asked her with hesitation.

"Sure."

"Thanks, and I'm Michael."

"I'm Valentines," she shot back.

"That's a nice name, it fits you perfectly." Knight made her smile.

"Thanks, so, what do you do for a living?" she said, hoping she didn't seem like the nosey type.

"I'm trying to get a club and I need a good partner to go half on it."

"Oh, cool, how are you going to afford a club?" She had a habit of asking a lot of questions since she was a kid.

"I recently got approved for a loan, so I'm using that business loan and all the money I saved up to open my dream club." Knight saw how impressed she looked.

"I went to school with a girl who opened a club in New Jersey. She is doing good, about to open another one," she said.

"What do you do for a living?" he asked.

"I'm sorry, I have to go, that's work calling. Take my number and maybe we can grab a bite to eat one day." She told him her number and left.

Knight locked the number in his phone and thought about how classy and cute the mystery woman was.

\*\*\*

Manhattan New York

Ms. Briscar let the young man into the condo she planned to sell for $1.7 million. As a real estate agent, she sold homes and condos throughout the week and got a 15% cut from every sale.

At 40, Ms. Briscar looked at least ten years younger because of clean eating. Bugatti Boy was her son, whom she didn't raise to be in the streets at all. It didn't make sense to her, because he had everything as a kid.

"This is the best condo on the block, sir. You have everything you need in a short walking distance," she said.

"What the rent looking like?" the man said

"Twenty-seven hundred a month," she told him, looking over the lease policy.

"Damn, that's high."

"Yeah, but it's well worth it. Let me show you the fancy bathroom I'm sure you will like. What happened to your wife? I thought you said she was coming to check on the place," the woman stated.

"She had to work, but I'm going to take some pictures for her," the man said.

"This is the bathroom." Ms. Briscar turned around to see a gun pointed at her face.

"You've been good to a guy, but the tour stops here," Baggs said with a look of malice.

Head waited for Baggs outside while he took care of Bugatti Boy's mom.

Days ago, Head saw Bugatti Boy and Ms. Briscar together and put two and two together.

"God bless your soul," Ms. Briscar said in fear.

*BOOM...*

*BOOM...*

*BOOM...*

Baggs left her body on the marble floor with three holes to her face, making a pool of blood.

Romell Tukes

# Chapter 11

The block had been doing numbers all day. Today all the crackheads got their welfare checks, so they were out early looking for drugs.

Mike's crew had already moved two and a half keys since 6 a.m., and it was now close to 1 p.m. He needed to go get some more work out of his stash in the building he trapped out of.

"I'm going to be right back in an hour. I'm going to cook up some work," Mike stated, walking across the street to a brick building with a ramp attached to it.

Mike hid three keys in the ceiling in the stairwell of the sixth floor. A fiend he knew cooked up the coke in a matter of minutes, and he knew what he was doing. Mike sold grams of hard to the fiends, and that's why they loved his crew and came from all over to see him.

Inside the stairway, Mike looked up and down the stairs to make sure nobody saw him go into his stash. He moved a ceiling piece, standing on his toes, and grabbed that black corner store bag full of coke.

Mike heard a noise and saw a Spanish brother rush in the stairway with a gun, catching him in the act.

"Drop the bag, nigga," Paco said to him smoothly.

Paco had been watching Mike since he saw him standing in the parking lot next to a nice car.

"Take it, man, please, I don't want no problems." Mike gave him the bag.

"What the fuck, is this it?" Paco's face frowned looking at three keys.

"Yeah, bro, I swear that's all I have."

"Give up that chain and watch too then, and if that shit ain't real, then I'm coming back," Paco said, taking the watch and chain, placing them in his pocket.

Paco jumped at Mike, who stumbled backwards, falling down the stairs, leaving Paco laughing as he left out the back of the building.

\*\*\*

Katosha Park, Bronx

Money got out of his car to see his boy Holiday awaiting him. Money reached out to Holiday on social media and set up a meeting date somewhere in the public.

The two knew each other since their days in jail as kids. Since he heard they were warring with the same people, he went to gather up some real soldiers so they could eliminate the ops.

"What's poppin', bro, good to see you." Money threw up his blood set with him before they took a walk side-by-side.

"Likewise, fam, I ain't know you was around my way, son. You should have reached out and I would've let you know how we rocking." Holiday knew Money was an official dude who had heart, and his name was heavy in Upstate Albany, Rochester, and Buffalo.

"Yeah, but I'm out here on a mission, and I believe we're on the same mission," Money told him.

"How is that?"

"I shot Lil' K in the head, but he survived to my knowledge. I'm out to kill Knight and his crew for the death of my father." Money's tone meant business, and Holiday saw the hunger in his eyes. He wanted blood.

"I'm sure you will be useful to me and Big Blazer."

"Hold on, useful? Nah, blood, I put in my own work. I just think if we come together we will get these niggas out the way, bro." Money didn't want him to get the wrong idea about why he was there.

"Okay, bro, that sounds good. When I get any scoops on these hoes ass niggas, I'll pull up on you, son. Word is bond, I got you," Holiday told him.

"Say less, I'm out, son, one." Money walked off.

Holiday called Big Blazer to tell him Money was now on board. Holiday knew Money had been in the Bronx because Fats told Big Blazer weeks ago when he came back from North Carolina.

\*\*\*

Uptown Bronx

Lil' K and Knight got down in the DMV, renewing their license and IDs under fake names and info.

"When Khalid is going to send that shit, bro?" Lil' K asked.

"Next week, nigga, we're moving his shit a hundred miles per hour, boy. That's shit like the early crack era." Knight couldn't believe Khalid's product was uncut and 100% pure, unlike Stephen's.

"We should have just robbed that nigga and killed his greedy ass." Lil' K stepped off the curb to a garage.

"Chill, son, I got a plan." Knight saw a car with tints rolling up on them, lowering its window.

*Bloc...*
*Bloc...*
*Bloc...*
*Bloc...*

The Honda did a drive-by but missed both men, racing off. Lil' K got his weapon out, but the car was already gone.

# Chapter 12

Pelham, BX

Lil' K made love to Red, giving her slow strokes, spreading her sex walls open.

"Uhmmmmmmmm, I love you," Red moaned, looking into his eyes while he fucked her missionary style.

Her pussy was so wet you could hear the loud, gushy noise all through the room. Lil' K went deep into her wet slit, fucking her so good she almost bit her bottom lip off. His balls drummed against her ass as she screamed and pleasured.

"I'm cumminngggg…" Red shouted so loud she hit a high note.

She raised her legs high up and took his whole rod before cum started to pour out her sex box like water. Lil' K pulled out, but he wasn't done. He flipped her on her stomach and slid into her from behind.

"When it's too much, let me know," he said, spreading her ass cheeks, grinding on her while she grabbed the Fendi sheets.

"Oh my god, fuck me daddy," she yelled until they both hit a high climax.

After sex, they sat up and talked about everything, like always.

"Everybody in Millbrooks got their issues?" Lil' K asked her.

"Yeah, they picked up everything a few days ago. Shit booming over there, baby." Red saw close to a half million in two weeks.

"Good, but I'ma see what we going do with this Big Blazer nigga," Lil' K told her.

"I know he sent Head to kill me. I remember dude's face, but I wonder how they got the drop on me." Red reminisced on the shootout that took place on Fordham Road and got upset.

"I'ma figure it out, you just focus on stacking the money," Lil' K said, as they cuddled in their new crib.

\*\*\*

## Manhattan, New York

Avona sat in Paco's car, watching him run into the store to grab some Dutch Masters to roll some fire weed in. When she called Paco two days ago, she was gassed because she had been waiting for his call since Summer Jam.

Tonight, they were going to Dave & Buster's to enjoy their first date. Paco came out of the store wearing Mike's chain and watch.

"What's up, ma." Paco got inside his Porsche with tints, pulling off.

"You, zaddy," Avona stated.

"Ok…" Paco saw she looked cute tonight in a dress and heels, showing her manicured toes.

"I want you to be mine, and you will, Pop."

"Facts?" Paco asked.

"I can show you better than I can tell you." Avona reached for his penis and got it out his Balmain jeans, slowly stroking it.

"That's how you feel?" Paco stopped at a traffic light and she threw his whole manhood in her wet mouth.

Avona popped her head up and down until they made it to the restaurant. By the time Paco pulled into the parking lot, he nutted twice in her mouth and she swallowed every drop.

"I got to keep you around. Damn, your head game is crazy, ma," Paco admitted, seeing cum around her thick lips.

"I can't wait until you fuck this pussy," she told him before getting out to go have a good time.

They spent the day getting to know each other, eating, and drinking, and then they went to fuck at her crib. Paco fucked her so good she saw stars and money.

Avona was hooked to Paco and he had no clue he just fucked a cold-blooded stalker.

\*\*\*

Soundview Bronx

The Soundview area of the Bronx had projects, regular buildings, and houses as well as a couple of stores almost on every corner.

Head and two of his workers posted up outside early on a paper chase. Chilling on the block wasn't Head's thing, but he had to pick up some money from his cousin, who been selling keys for him.

"It's too early, fam, to be out here," one of Head's workers told him, sitting on two crates on the wall.

"Early bird gets the worm," Head said, smoking a cigarette, watching two people in hoodies walk up the block, and one of them was shaped like a woman. He came to his senses quickly and pulled his weapon out at the same time as Red and Bugatti Boy.

*Bloc, Bloc, Bloc, Bloc, Bloc, Bloc, Bloc...*

Head ran off, shooting, leaving his two goons to die with no weapon as he took off down the block ducking bullets.

Romell Tukes

# Chapter 13

Highbridge, Bronx

Kazzy and Lil' K sat behind the wheel of a truck, watching an apartment where Holiday's mom lived.

"You sure that's the spot, bro? Because if this nigga getting all that money, why is his mother living in the trap?" Lil' K said, looking out the window.

"You know how niggas be, they get rich and forget about their family and loved ones, bro. That's why I love our family." Kazzy stood on the value of family.

"That's a big fact, Loc, but not to get off topic, why did you turn crip and everybody in the city blood?" Lil' K asked a question he always wanted to know.

Lil' K and Kazzy liked spending brotherly time with each other. It was just like their younger days.

"I just wanted to be different, cuz. All three of us are different, bro. Knight got a diamond grill, I'm crippin', and you are a mastermind. I can't front. When you were hitting my spot, I ain't know who it was, fam." Kazzy thought about when he heard of Lil' K's crew out turning up the city.

"I just wanted to prove a point and show you I am a savage too and can hold my own. When Mommy died, I felt like it was time for me to come out of my shell," Lil' K stated.

A woman wearing an Old Navy hoodie carrying a store bag walked into the build. They assumed she was Holiday's mom, so they got out the car, following her inside the building

Holiday's mom, Maxy, walked in her building, tapping her foot on the floor, geeking for another hit of coke. Maxy had a bad coke habit and she lived a fast life. Every night she had to party and turn up.

She also had her a young nigga she'd been fucking for a couple of months now, and he waited upstairs for her, taking a nap in her crib.

Maxy turned around to see two young men behind her coming into the building. She wanted to flirt with one of them but when she saw the guns appear from behind their backs, she slowly walked off.

"Hold on, shorty." Kazzy stopped her in her tracks.

"Oh, me?" Maxy knew Holiday got her into this, so she knew she had to get herself out of it.

"You know why we're here?" Lil' K saw she was about to say something.

"Holiday with Houston, his baby mama." Maxy thought that's what the goons wanted.

"Thanks," Kazzy said to her before he squeezed the trigger.

*Boc...*

*Boc...*

*Boc...*

Maxy's body flew into the elevator as it opened, leaving her dead on the elevator floor. When the doors closed, the elevator went to the fourth floor as the men left the building.

\*\*\*

Uptown Bronx

Knight walked through a small shopping center to pay his phone bill at a phone store. Walking past the store, he saw the woman he saw in SoHo named Valentines. She looked sexier than the last time.

There was a flower shop next door to the phone store where Valentines was paying her phone bill. Knight ran into the flower shop and grabbed dozens of multicolored, beautiful, fresh-cut, long-stem roses.

He paid for the flowers and went into the phone store, creeping up behind this woman. When Valentines turned around, she saw the man who presented himself as Michael weeks ago at a restaurant.

"These are for you, beautiful." Knight handed her the flowers and saw her smiling hard.

"This is so sweet, thank you." She saw the store employees were watching her, as if Knight was about to propose too.

"Long time no speak."

"I know, but I've been so busy," she told him.

"I understand."

"Why'd you never call me, Michael?" She gave him a disappointed look.

"I've been busy," Knight shot back.

"Now you are using my line?"

"Facts, but are you busy? There's a pizza shop next door. If you down, let's go get a slice of pizza," Knight asked.

"I have an hour break. I'm down, Michael." Valentines left the phone store and Knight didn't even pay his own phone bill.

Romell Tukes

# Chapter 14

Soundview, Bronx

Holiday called Money and asked him to meet him at a local park so he could fill him in on what was going on.

Yesterday, Holiday attended his mom Maxy's funeral, and it took a toll on him. He wanted blood for his mom's death. His little sister, Avona, cried for days. His mom wasn't always the best mom, but she did her best when he was growing up.

Money leaned on a green Audi, fresh off a car lot.

"Yo, what's poppin', my G." Money embraced Holiday, who was looking around to make sure no police were watching because lately, the boys were following him around.

"I'm blessed, bro, but I got word these niggas opening shop all around town, from Millbrook to Uptown, so we can hit all their people until someone gives us some information" Holiday told Money, and it was like music to his ears.

"When you going to be ready to bust a move?" Money had been impatient lately.

"Soon, fam."

Lil' K and Knight watched Holiday and Money talk from a distance.

"That's him," Lil' K said, staring at Money as if he knew him.

"Who?" Knight shot back, wondering what they were talking about.

"Son with the red shirt is the one who shot me in the head." Lil' K remembered Money.

Lil' K thought about Money's face every night in his dreams.

"What are you waiting for then?" Knight said those words, and Lil' K already had the van door open.

Knight heard this park was a Holiday and Head hangout spot, so they'd been staking it out now for a few hours a day.

*Boc...*

*Boc...*

*Boc...*

*Tatt...*

*Tatt...*

*Tatt...*

Money and Holiday dove on the floor and got to their weapons, as the kids and parents ran everywhere, trying to save their own lives.

*Bloc...*

*Bloc...*

Holiday fired back, hitting an old man in a wheelchair twice.

Lil' K caught Holiday in his left shoulder, seeing him lean on a car while Money let off round after round at both of the gunmen.

A park patrol officer yelled for Knight to freeze, but that only made Knight mad, and he shot at him, killing him.

*Boc...*

*Boc...*

*Boc...*

Money and Holiday jumped in Holiday's car and rushed out the lot, speeding off while bullets hit the back of the car trunk.

Lil' K and Knight got in the van, leaving out in the opposite direction before the police showed up.

\*\*\*

Cortland Projects, Bronx

Bugatti Boy and his little brother, Abraham, walked out of the back building on their way to go to Six Flags in New Jersey.

After his mom's body was found in a condo, he had to raise his little brother with the help of his aunt. His little brother took their mom's death harder than Bugatti. To be only 12 years old, Abraham was very smart.

"Where are we going?" Abraham asked.

"It's a surprise," Bugatti told him.

"Okay."

*BOOM...*

*BOOM...*

*BOOM...*

*BOOM...*

*BOOM...*

Bugatti Boy looked at shooters creeping up on him from the car lot and let go.

*Boc...*

*Boc...*

*Boc...*

Bugatti sprayed back at them but missed by far. Ducking, he looked at his lil' brother who was laying on the floor in a puddle of blood.

"Nooooooo..." Bugatti Boy shouted then popped up blasting non-stop, hitting one of the shooters.

Baggs went toe-to-toe with Bugatti Boy until they both ran out of bullets.

Shells were everywhere on the floor before all of them took off, leaving two dead bodies on the ground.

***

Harlem, New York

Time wasn't on 6'7's side, because he had two more days to bring down a crew, and his brother blocked his number. He knew a couple of Harlem cats who worked for Holiday, so he reached out to them. Walking into the building, he made his way to the eighth floor.

6'7 knocked three times when he got to the door, which was the special knock.

"6'7, what's shakin', boy, come in." A fat nigger answered the door to let 6'7 inside to see his brother, Nails.

When 6'7 walked into the apartment, he saw Nails and Holiday standing there with guns, as if they were waiting on someone.

"What's poppin', bro?" 6'7 looked at Holiday.

"Have a seat, bro." Holiday pulled a seat out for him.

"What's going on?" 6'7 said, sitting down.

"Nigger, shut the fuck up. What you telling the police?"

"Police?" 6'7 played dumb until a bullet hit his upper thigh.

"Ahhhhhhh… Okayyy," 6'7 screamed in pain.

"I know you called me trying to line me up. You sounded too fishy, so I called Holiday and he gave me the rundown." Nails stood in front of 6'7's face.

"I'm sorry, man, I fucked up," 6'7 cried.

"What did you say?" Holiday stated.

"Well, you blocked me, so I had to find someone else," he admitted.

"I knew it… that's what they've been telling me all over the place. I can't believe you would have given up your own blood."

"I fucked up bad, bro." 6'7 had tears in his eyes.

"Rat ass nigger," Nails mumbled.

*Bloc…*

*Bloc…*

*Bloc…*
*Bloc…*
Holiday shot 6'7 in his forehead then left.

\*\*\*

Queens New York

Paco waited in line at KFC, staring at a woman with a fat ass, which was sitting perfect in her jeans, and a cute face. He had somewhere to be, so he pulled out a pen and napkin and wrote her a small note with his name and number.

Paco got back in line and discreetly placed the napkin inside the woman's Fendi handbag. After she ordered her food she caught his eye but tried not to look thirsty as she put an extra strut in her walk for him while leaving.

Romell Tukes

# Chapter 15

Manhattan, New York

"Ugghhhh, shhh," Valentines moaned as Knight held her against the bathroom in the hotel while the shower water hit his back.

Her pussy was so tight and warm. Knight couldn't go as deep into her as he wanted.

"Oh my god," she screamed in pain and pleasure. A nigga ain't beat her walls down like this in a long time, so she was head over heels. "I'm cumming," she moaned with her legs wrapped around his waist.

"Say my name," Knight whispered into her ear.

"Michael… Ugghhhh…" she screamed, squirting all over his manhood and pelvis area.

Knight had no clue she was a squirter. Seeing her squirt mix in with the shower was sexy, so he bent her over and fucked her doggystyle, killing her shit until she came back to back.

The date night they had turned into a fuck fest. It was going down all night in the hotel.

***

Soundview, Bronx

Holiday and BeBe laid in the bed, looking at the ceiling, out of breath.

"Damn, you make a bitch go crazy." BeBe had been at Holiday's crib all night, making love to him.

The two had been dating for a couple of weeks and everything was perfect. They were spending a lot of time with each other.

Holiday loved everything about BeBe. She was bad, real, and beautiful.

"I heard that one before, ma, big facts," he told her, pillow talking.

"I bet you did, but I have to, boo. I'm calling you tomorrow, but you need to clean this place," she said, getting out of bed to get dressed to go home.

"That's what I got you for." Holiday threw a pillow at her, making her laugh.

***

Brooklyn, New York

The three men all stood under the Brooklyn Bridge talking and putting their plans together to corner the market. Fats, Big Blazer, and Money sat in a circle, smoking blunts of loud.

"Money, I need you to be more active in Brooklyn and let Big Blazer and his crew take care of that shit in the Bronx," Fats stated.

"That's not going to work, but I can bounce back and forth until I find these niggars," Money stated, not feeling what Fats was saying.

"We need Money in the Bronx, Fats. You wilding, bro. Boy about that action. You worried about Money and we worried about making it alive every day," Big Blazer said, speaking the truth because he and his crew were in the streets.

"We need to get rid of this nigga Knight," Fats said, exhausted.

"We're going to get him," Money stated.

"You got that shipment ready for my man, Fats?" Money asked.

"I'mma be ready in a few days, but y'all need to get rid of that headache. He fucking business up."

"I heard he was flooding the whole Uptown with some fire coke and dope," Big Blazer stated.

"So I heard," Fats said, sounding upset.

"We're going to handle it, Fats," Money said before leaving.

\*\*\*

Brooklyn New York

Red walked through the Barclays Center, which was packed with people who came out for a big rap concert. She followed a cute brown-skin chick to a small bar on the lower level.

The woman she followed for an hour was Money's baby mother, which Lil' K found out. The woman they called Chanel B used to be a bartender at a couple of big-name clubs in the city.

"Hi." Red sat next to the woman in order to get some drinks.

"Nice bag," Chanel B told her, looking at Red's Chanel bag and how pretty she looked tonight. Chanel B went both ways. She liked men and women, and Red was her type.

"Thanks, what's your name and why you alone?" Red asked her.

"Chanel B is what everybody calls me, but I'm just chilling."

"I know the vibes," Red stated, getting her drink.

The two women were chilling and vibing all night until Chanel B had to go home and get ready for work before dropping her son off at her mom's crib. She was unaware Red had been tailing her all the way to her job.

Romell Tukes

# Chapter 16

Elmira Prison, NY

Less did his last set of pull-ups in the gym area filled with other prisoners.

There was a big basketball game on the court, but Less stopped playing jail basketball months ago after he got into two fights over a basketball game in the big gym.

Since he was in prison, he gained close to 30 pounds of muscle from doing weight lifting.

Prison took a toll on him emotionally but mentally, he strengthened day by day, and he took in everything around him as a tool to never come back to prison.

"What's popping, MackBaller? I see you in here getting to a bag," a big muscle-head gang member said, lifting hundred-pound dumbbells.

"I'm straight, son, in here trying to get this shit out, you heard." Less got under the flat bench and lifted 200 pounds with ease.

There were over 25 big, stocky niggars in the gym in tank tops, exercising, sweating, and watching other niggas workout.

"I'm out of here, son. They about to call early to go back." Less got up and left the gym.

"Youngin' wait for me," an old head yelled, making his way through the crowd of people trying to leave the gym to go back to their units.

"OG Bobby, where you been? I was waiting for you before I left the block, but you weren't in your crib," Less referred to his cell as his crib.

Over the intercom, they heard B block inmates had five minutes to get back to the housing unit.

OG Bobby had been locked up close to 20 years in New York State Prison, doing a life sentence with no chance of parole. He was a true OG from Brooklyn and well-respected with a crazy body count. Growing up, OG Bobby worked as a hitman.

When he was arrested, the DA charged him with seven murders and five attempted murders. At trial, he had eight star witnesses, and most of them were rats he did work for or grew up with.

"I had to get me a game of chess in with a good comrade," OG Bobby told him, walking back to their unit.

"Okay, I thought you wanted to hit that pull-up bar."

"Do I look like I need a pull-up bar?" OG Bobby flexed his muscles in his shirt. He was cut up and lean for a nigga his age, because he worked out six days a week.

"You got that, OG." Less laughed.

"I got a greeting card from one of my rats who put me in here. That shit hurt like a nigga shitting out bricks," OG Bobby told Less.

"Damn, boy, niggas vicious out there."

"You have no clue, and I heard this nigger Fats out there touched a million." OG Bobby never really talked about his case or lifestyle he lived in the streets.

"Fats?" Less knew there had to be another Fats in New York than his ops.

"Yeah, this fat bitch is a plug and he took the stand on me, my main witness. Have you heard of him?" OG Bobby saw a funny look on his face.

"That's son me and my bros got beef with," Less told him.

"Wow, small world. I did a lot of work for that snitch nigga, and he told on four bodies." OG Bobby shook his head, walking to his cell. They changed the topic and talked about a couple of new rappers taking the game.

\*\*\*

West Burnside, Bronx

Kazzy and Red kept a close eye on the barbershop Baggs and his homies were at, with a child Baggs had with him.

"What's up with you?" Kazzy asked Red, seeing her mind had been elsewhere lately.

"I'm straight, bro, focused on getting these niggas out the way. I can't even enjoy the summer. I'm mad that my period is on, so I can't make 'salat' prayer for Muslims," Red spilled everything on him.

"Damn, too much info."

"You asked," replied Red.

In the next instant, their target exited the store. Moving quickly, Kazzy and Red hopped out of the car with their glizzys out and ready to go the fuck off.

*Bloc...*

*Bloc...*

*Bloc...*

*Bloc...*

One of Baggs' homies tried to go bullet for bullet with Kazzy, until two rounds lifted him off his feet. Red fired two shots at Baggs, but his son jumped in the crossfire, catching both bullets.

When Baggs saw that, his heart dropped. Police sirens could be heard, so Red and Kazzy knew it was time to go. Baggs ran up the street. He was still on parole and wasn't going back to prison.

Romell Tukes

# Chapter 17

Uptown, NY

Lil' K and Bugatti Boy had a nigga tied up in zip ties in the back of a big commercial van parked behind an abandoned alley.

They caught one of Holiday's workers outside of a bar near Boston Road and snatched him.

"Don't kill me, brotty. I'll tell you whatever y'all need, please," Lil' Vic said, unable to move in the back of the van on the floor.

"Where can I find them dumb niggas. We know you work for them, but where they at?" Lil' K had been running out of patience all day, just riding around looking for Holiday's people.

"Head's pops lives two blocks away on 719 Howard Street. He is dying of cancer, on bed rest. I bring his dad food for him," Lil' Vic admitted.

"What do you know about Holiday, fam?" Bugatti Boy asked.

"I only saw him twice, bro. I just started working. I hate them niggas, let me help y'all set them up," Lil' Vic said, looking at both men, hoping this would save him.

"Nah, fam." Lil' K pulled out a zip tie and placed it around his neck, choking the life out of Lil' Vic, literally.

After tossing Lil' Vic's body behind a gas station, they drove to Head's dad's crib.

"You know that bullshit you did in Africa was corny as hell, bro. You could have got everybody killed," Lil' K said.

"Nigga, I ain't know shit about that, fam. They kidnapped me too, bro. I will never double-cross y'all, factz. This is a big chance for us to lock down the Bronx the right way." Bugatti Boy drove the van.

"Nigga, we jack boys, that's our life, bro. Selling drugs is our day job, son, and don't forget that," Lil' K said while seeing Head's dad's house in the middle of row houses lined up on the dark, quiet block.

"Y'all got my loyalty, bro. We family, and y'all my day ones," Bugatti Boy told him from his heart.

Bugatti Boy knew the crew looked at him differently since coming back from the motherland, but he didn't know his dad either until that trip.

He didn't give a fuck about Khalid being his dad or about his money. Bugatti Boy's loyalty was to his crew.

Losing his mom took a toll on him, but he held it down and used his pain as a reason to kill shit.

Getting out the van, they planned how they were going to get inside the crib.

"Window it is. You got to give me a boost, bro." Lil' K got to the side of the crib, reaching for the house window.

"Come on, step on my back, bro, and be careful. My shit hurt, boy." Bugatti Boy got on all fours so Lil' K could step on his back for a boost.

"Ahh, shit," Bugatti mumbled while Lil' K put a ton of pressure on his back.

Lil' K got in the window easier than he thought because the latch on the inside wasn't fully locked.

Lil' K snuck through the dark crib, and the clock on the wall read 3:10 a.m. He knew the man would be sleep.

The crib was small. Lil' K walked into the first room to see a man laying on his back, hooked up to a machine and oxygen tank.

Hearing a noise, Lil' K looked back and saw Bugatti Boy behind him.

"The front door was open the whole time," Bugatti Boy said, shaking his head.

"Shhhhh…" Lil' K aimed the gun at the old man's head.

*Bloc…*

*Bloc…*

*Bloc…*

*Bloc…*

The lights from the gunfire light up the whole room.

Leaving the house, they saw an old guard dog and shot him twice as they left out the back entrance.

\*\*\*

South Bronx, New York
Two Days Later

Red's mom, Kendra, walked out her job at the clinic, tired from the long day of work. Kendra looked like beautiful eye candy. Every man she bypassed, she cast a spell on.

When she lost Banger to the streets, she begged Red to leave the game alone, but they ended up in a bad argument.

Opening the driver's door to her Range, a man with a crazy look on his face approached her. Kendra had some stalkers, but she didn't know this man from a can of paint.

"You okay, sir?" she asked, then saw his gun, thinking it was a robbery, so she ran in her high heels until two bullets hit her in the back, taking her out..

Head stood over her, firing two more bullets in her face for the death of his pops.

Romell Tukes

# Chapter 18

Canaan USP Prison, PA

Knight made sure he had his ID on him and all the information he needed to visit his boy, D Fatal Brim.

Last week, the federal prison just accepted his visiting form he sent to the prison so he could visit. Today was D Fatal Brim's birthday, so he had wanted to pop up and show him some love.

Walking into the front entrance of the prison, he saw correctional officers chewing on tobacco, the same shit he saw when he did prison time in VA.

Looking around, he saw shit that looked so familiar. Coming back to jail wasn't an option for Knight. He planned to go all out in the midst.

Knight gave the CO at the front desk his ID and got searched, then went to the visit room, waiting for his boy to come down.

D Fatal Brim popped another mint in his mouth, trying to take away the liquor smell. He was on his unit drinking white lightning, which was a prison drink made from wine, or some would call it hooch.

The inmates would cook the wine and it would turn into a strong vodka type of drink. D Fatal Brim drunk a whole quart of the vodka-type drink to the head, which was close to 80% proof.

Walking to the visit, he didn't know who was there to see him. Seconds later, he stepped foot on the visit room floor and he saw Knight sitting there, which made him smile.

"Big bro." Knight saw D Fatal Brim had put on some muscle and cuts.

"What's poppin'?"

"You," Knight shot back, seeing he'd been drinking and he smelled it on his breath.

"Just doing hard time, my G, good to see you in person," D Fatal Brim stated.

"Happy birthday, nigga, you know I had to pull up on you."

"Thanks, I've been getting visits, but I recently bagged a Spanish joint on a dating site, and shit been looking good." D Fatal Brim smiled, thinking about the woman.

"That's good, bro, because a nigga be needing some rec behind these walls, son." Knight knew how it felt to have no bitches once you got locked up.

Knight lost all his hoes when he went to prison, but when he got out, they all came back running.

The visit lasted an hour then Knight had to leave, but he made plans to visit his brother again soon. Outside, he looked through his phone and saw that he had 16 missed calls.

He had his phone down, so he couldn't see the car pulling behind him as he walked past a CO going to work.

*Bloc...*

*Bloc...*

*Bloc...*

*Bloc...*

The gunfire made Knight take cover like he was in Iraq. The CO got shots to the chest. Knight's weapon was in his car at the end of the parking lot. Money and his goons spun the light trying to catch Knight, but he was too fast.

A couple of correctional officers shot at Money's car and took out the car window. Money knew he had to get low and out of PA, because the stolen car was now hot.

Knight made it to his luxury car and dipped off so he wouldn't be questioned about what happened.

"How the fuck he catch me lackin'?" Knight asked himself all the way back to New York.

***

## Bronx, New York

Red drove her candy red Range Rover Sport SUV on her way to pick up some money from her crew of workers in Michelle projects.

Since the death of her mom, it took a lot out of her not to kill every soul she believed had any dealings with the ops. Lil' K provided comfort to her, but that really wasn't enough. She needed to raise the murder rate.

She listened to Monica's old album, trying to clear her mind. She needed a vacation. She and Lil' K talked about going to the Middle East to learn more about the Islam religion.

Romell Tukes

# Chapter 19

New Rochelle, New York

Head followed the new-model Kia Sedan into a classy neighborhood outside the Bronx in a county called Westchester.

Holiday sat in the passenger seat texting his girlfriend and baby mother, Houston, who was texting him demanding money so she could go out.

"Yooooo…" Head shouted over the loud music.

"What's poppin'?"

"You think son is really down with us or he's just trying to get in the loop?" Head asked, referring to Money, who he disliked.

"Son official, Head, I would never bring a nigga into our circle unless I knew he could benefit us." Holiday knew Head was concerned because a lot of dudes had hidden agendas of why they wanted to get down.

Holiday didn't trust a soul, but he knew in life, you have to take risks. He knew who a person was when they stood tall during war, and Money was there head first and frontline, so that said enough for him and Big Blazer.

"Aight." Head parked across the street from a dorm on a college campus.

"What are we doing here, son? I got shit to do". Holiday thought they were going to Yonkers so he could pick up some money from his homie who moved keys for him.

"Be patient, I got the drop on one of the ops peoples," Head said, thinking about when he recently had to bury his father.

Head's dad had only a few weeks to live anyway due to the cancer that spread through his body.

"Hurry up, bro, damn, it's almost 11 p.m." Holiday checked this watch.

Ten minutes later, Head saw two people walking out the door and jumped out the car.

"Wait here," Head told him with his gun out.

Holiday watched Head creep into the college dorm parking lot. When Holiday saw the two people in the street, he couldn't believe his eyes.

He saw BeBe with another woman, walking to the Kia. When he got out to stop Head, it was too late. He saw BeBe's body drop.

*Boc...*

*Boc...*

*Boc...*

*Boc...*

Head dashed back to the car, looking at Holiday.

"Get in the car," Head told Holiday, seeing a crazy look in his eyes.

They drove off speeding into the college campus.

"Nigga, why you killed my girlfriend?" Holiday got his gun from underneath the seat, thinking Head was on some double-cross shit.

"That bitch is Knight's sister."

"What?"

"Yeah, the one in the red. I've been watching her for a few weeks since I saw her with Knight, but I lost Knight and tailed her. Hold on, blood, that was your girlfriend? The bitch you've been telling me about?" Head couldn't believe Holiday's words.

Holiday couldn't even speak. He never even took the time to look into her family ties, which could have been his downfall.

\*\*\*

Bronx, New York
Meanwhile

Houston went inside the 24-hour store to buy some cigarettes. She just got off of work from doing overtime. It was close to midnight and she couldn't wait to get home to go to sleep.

She texted her baby daddy, Holiday, for some money, but he texted back talking spicy to her. Tomorrow night, she had plans to get up with Big Blazer and fuck the shit out of him to get back at Holiday.

Coming out of the store, she ran into a bad bitch who looked exotic. Houston never dealt with another woman sexually, but this bitch would turn the Virgin Mary on.

When Houston turned her head, a bullet slammed right into her brain, killing her. The block was dark and empty, so Red took her time hopping on her motorcycle, pulling off.

Riding down the street, an NYPD cop car emerged from a side block, catching her speeding. Red swiftly slipped out her weapon.

*Bloc…*
*Bloc…*
*Bloc…*
*Bloc…*

Red emptied the whole clip into the cop's face, killing him, before speeding off to a dark side block.

Romell Tukes

# Chapter 20

### Williamsbridge, Bronx

Baggs pulled out his baby mother's parking lot on his way to Soundview to meet up with Big Blazer. They were having a big party for the death of Lil' Blazer.

Williamsbridge was a nice area in the Bronx near the 6 train. Baggs had been trying to rebuild a new relationship with his baby mother since they recently lost one of their children due to violence from his street beef.

Baggs' baby mother had a good job as an RN. She was a fat white woman with a lot of money. His whole bid, she rode it out and held him down. That's why he had so much respect for her, unlike most women who left their loved ones for dead as soon as they got a sentence.

Bugatti Boy and Knight saw Baggs' car race off down the block, which fucked up their plans.

"Dammit. I knew he was leaving," Knight shouted, with a small box in his hand.

"Fuck it, we can still try this shit out to see if it's official," Bugatti Boy said, looking at the box in Knight's hand.

Khalid knew a terrorist Islamic leader who had a nephew in Queens who made bombs, so he sent Bugatti to him just in case he needed his help one day.

"Facts, you going to do it?" Knight asked.

Bugatti took the box and ran across the street with a hoodie on in broad day. He sat the box on the front porch and rang the doorbell before running off.

Once Bugatti was back in the car, Knight hit the pedal and saw a fat white bitch open the door. Bugatti Boy followed the instructions the man gave him and pushed the button on the remote two times.

The explosion was so bad, the whole block shook like one big earthquake just hit.

"Damn, boy." Knight saw the scene from his rearview mirror and told Bugatti to call the Muslim terrorist back so they could load up on some more TNT shit.

\*\*\*

161st Courthouse, BX

Detective Valentines had to come to court today so she could speak in front of a judge to get six warrants for a couple of known gang leaders who had been getting people killed for close to a year now.

The crew's name was called SMM for The Soundview area and the Castle Hill projects area. Getting the warrants signed off was the hardest thing, because if she didn't have evidence to build a strong case with the judge, then it would be worthless.

Knight texted her good morning and she replied. The two talked about moving in with each other, but she told him to wait until she got a little more comfortable with him. The sex between them had her head over heels, but she knew there was more to a relationship than sex. She felt like there was a lot more she needed to learn about him.

Detective Valentines went to see the judge, and he turned her down, saying she didn't have enough proof to charge the six gang leaders with any type of murders.

\*\*\*

Mount Vernon, New York

Lil' K and Red were at Jumar (Muslim Service) outside of the Bronx, because they ain't want to get caught slippin'.

Both of them took their religion very seriously and focused on Allah and learning all the ins and outs of their Dean.

Growing up in a Christian household was all about church and Jesus for them both. When they found Islam, it took their heart and they felt like it was only right to devote themselves.

Learning Arabic was the only hard part, because they had to say their prayer in Arabic, which was the chapter out of the Qur'an in Arabic.

They sat in the mosque listening to every word that Imam spoke in a stern, clear pitch. After service, they took off the Islamic attire and went to the Bronx. They saw two of Big Blazer's workers selling work on the corner and sprayed 20 rounds, killing them both.

Lil' K and Red made it back home right on time for ASR, afternoon prayer.

Romell Tukes

# Chapter 21

Bronx, New York

Paco drove his Range into the Parkchester section on his way towards D'Aray's crib.

He met D'Aray weeks ago in Queens when he put his number on a napkin and slipped it into her purse. That same night, they talked and got to know each other. They'd been focused on building a friendship, but D'Aray wanted him to come over for Netflix movies.

The town had been turned up the past couple of weeks, so Paco had been spending a lot of time in Washington Heights checking in on his traps. He also opened a shop in Harlem on a block called Broadway, which was known for its drug traffic area.

Paco pulled into a small driveway and looked at a two-story house. He looked at the new Lexus Coupe, wondering if it was D'Aray. He grabbed his pistol from the stash, hiding it in his back before exiting the truck, knowing bitches wasn't shit.

Knocking on the door, he heard her voice in the background, and seconds later, the door flew open and D'Aray stood in booty shorts and a sports bra, showing her flat stomach.

"Paco." She hugged him tightly.

"Hey, sexy," he replied, feeling her soft brown skin. When she stepped back, he peeped how fat her pussy print was and couldn't believe it.

"Come inside, are you hungry? I'll cook or order you some food," she asked, locking her door.

Paco saw how laced her pad was and he had to give it to her. It looked like she spent a pretty penny on her shit.

"I'm good, I ate earlier," he said, following her into the kitchen.

"Okay, I got a couple of bottles of D'ussé, Moet, and Dom P, so pick your poison." D'Aray bent over, giving him a full view of her fat ass.

"D'ussé vibes," he shot back.

"Big facts, we going to my room," she said and led him to the back. "How about we watch *Set It Off*. That's my favorite movie." She handed him the bottle and got under the covers in her queen-size bed.

"I'm with you, drink?" Paco popped open the bottle.

"I don't drink, but take off your shoes and pull up," she told him, seeing him waste no time as the movie started.

Paco's rod grew as he climbed into the bed with her before putting the bottle on the dresser. When they cuddled, he slid his finger towards her coochie, but she stopped him.

"I'm on red."

"Huh?"

"I'm on my period." She saw the look on his face and if looks could kill, she would be dead.

"It's cool." Paco kissed her lips.

"But I can do something special for you," she said, going under the covers. She started to give him head, going crazy in his lap, making him tap out back to back as he busted off in her throat.

Paco ended up watching a couple of movies with her and falling asleep, waking up to more oral sex and breakfast in bed.

\*\*\*

Miami Beach, Florida

Stephen swam laps in her pool after the workout she had with her fitness trainer. Staying in shape nowadays to her was everything, and she loved her nice ass and flat abs.

Her Miami Beach mansion was so big somebody would get lost in it. At times, she had a lot of friends, so she would do all types of parties.

In an hour from now, she had a meeting with one of her clients from Philly. Stephen wanted to rage war on Khalid for taking Knight from her, but she knew he had a cousin in South Florida selling work out there for him, so she had a plan.

If he had the nerve to stop her money, then she would return the favor.

Romell Tukes

# Chapter 22

Soundview, Bronx

The heat wave across the city today gave people warnings to stay inside, but everybody in Soundview was out and about.

Holiday loved being in the hood. This was home for him and his crew. No matter how rich he got, he never planned to abandon his hood.

Head and Baggs were out of town in Vermont getting money, setting up shop selling grams for triple the going rate in the Bronx.

"What's poppin', Classic," Holiday told an old head who was posted up on the wall chilling, spitting game to a couple of young women.

Classic had been pimpin' for over twenty-eight years. He was really self-made and a millionaire. He came back to his old hood to find new talent, as he called it.

"I'm groovy, just trying to get my feet wet without draining it under the—"

*Tat...*

*Tat...*

*Tat...*

*Tat...*

*Tat...*

Holiday tried to run back in the building, but he didn't realize he was hit until he made it in the elevator. Two bullets entered his right upper thigh. His auntie was a licensed nurse and lived on the seventh floor, so he knew she was the only option.

Four of his goons laid out on the front deck in a pool of blood on the hottest day of the summer.

Knight and Lil' K drove the bikes to a small garage, Uptown next to Eastchester Gardens where Lil' K and Bugatti Boy lived.

They parked the bikes and shut them off.

"I know I got him, but I don't. I think it was a good shot, son," Knight said, leaving the helmet on the back.

Lil' K walked to his G wagon shaking his head, because Knight lost his touch.

"Bro, we had that nigga dead-ass lined up until you fucked it up," Lil' K stated.

"Stop trippin', will get him." Knight knew Lil' K was in his bag about BeBe's death and so was he, but he knew Karma played by its own rules.

\*\*\*

## Little Italy, Bronx

Mike found a new area to hustle at, which he'd been making more money at anyway. When Kazzy robbed him, he knew there was no way he was going back over there to lose his life.

The block had been dry all day, so Mike walked to his car, on his way to Long Island to meet up with a bad snow bunny he met weeks ago in a club.

Walking down the block, he saw a bad bitch with a sexy walk coming his way. When he saw her face, he had to stop her. There was no way he would let her walk past.

"Damn, ma, what's the vibes?"

"You know the vibes," she said.

"Where you headed? I'm trying to get up with you, ma."

"Oh, is that right?"

"Facts." Mike knew he had her now.

"What's your math?" She went in her Louis Vuitton purse and pulled out a gun, taking him by surprise.

*BOOM!*

*BOOM!*

*BOOM!*

Red shot him in his forehead, then Kazzy pulled up on the street for her and she got inside.

Romell Tukes

# Chapter 23

### South Africa

Khalid walked into his large dining room in his Islamic garment.

Two of his wives sat at the table awaiting their husband. Khalid's other two wives lived in his other mansion in a small village.

"As-salam-alakum," both of his wives said before he sat down.

"Wa'alaikum salaom, go get my dinner," Khalid told them both.

His wives got up and went to the kitchen to get his food they prepared for him earlier. Khalid's table was full of fruit and bread like the Last Supper.

Eating like a king and living like a king was all he knew. He liked his food well done, especially his meat, and everybody knew his pet peeve.

Minutes later, both of his wives came out with his food trays full of everything from meat to stews.

"Thank you." Khalid began with his meat and saw there was a little pink in the center of his steak.

Khalid stopped eating, and his wives did at the same time.

"Who made this?" Khalid looked at both of his wives.

"Me." Yemena raised her hand, a little nervous.

Yemena was the youngest and newest wife he had, and her beauty stood out from all of them.

"Come here, so I can show you."

"Ok." Yemena saw Khalid's other wife close her eyes, as if she was saying a silent prayer.

When Yemena got close enough, Khalid grabbed the back of her neck with his right hand and stabbed her in the neck until blood squirted everywhere.

Khalid tossed her body on the floor as if nothing happened.

"Eat," he told his wife, who shed a tear for the woman she had many threesomes with.

\*\*\*

Bronx, New York

Club Salsa Con Fuego had rap, R&B night live tonight, and Red enjoyed herself with Chanel B. The two women danced, having a good time. They looked like a badass gay couple.

Chanel B danced for close to an hour, then she went to take a seat and Red trailed behind her.

"Oh my god," Chanel B shot with a slur because she was drunk.

"This shit is lit tonight." Red they took a sip of water from a glass cup that I already had her red lipstick on it.

"Facts, you looking good too." Chanel B didn't realize how close her and Red's face was.

Caught in the moment, both women found themselves kissing and fondling each other's breasts. Red pulled back when she realized what she was really doing.

"I have to go." Red got up to leave and Chanel B went after her, but Red was long gone, using a tactic she found in *The Art of Seduction*.

\*\*\*

City Island Seafood, Bronx

Knight and Paco came out to a seafood place on the long strip full of seafood restaurants and water.

"Yo, this place is new. I've never been here," Paco stated, looking around at the crowded place and smelling the good fried food.

"I ain't been out here in years, boy, but I'm pulling up out here more, and they got some bad bitches," Knight shot back, looking around.

"Who you fucking with, son? I ain't seen you with no bitches yet. Normally, you stay with a J-Lo in the cut." Paco saw Knight's grill light up.

"Chill, son, I can't spill the beans," Knight stated.

"Here we go," Paco added.

"Naw, bro, me and shorty just vibing, facts." Knight talked about ValentinesValentine for the first time.

"Ok, I'm fucking with some bad bitches, bro." Paco got their food and they made their way outside.

They ran right into Money and Holiday, laughing. When both crews ran into each other, it was an onsite. Knight got to his gun first.

*Bloc...*

*Bloc...*

*Bloc...*

Everybody backpedaled as they fired at each other.

*Boc...*

*Boc...*

Paco hit Holiday in his shoulder and he hit a civilian, who was an off-duty detective, killing him.

Money and Knight got lost in the crowd as people ran all over the place, making it hard for anyone to get a good shot.

Knight and Paco blended in with the crowd of civilians.

Romell Tukes

# Chapter 24

### Bronx, New York

Detective Valentines got a call about a witness who had to speak to her about a murder she saw last night in front of her building.

There was a war going on in the Bronx with the YGS and Macks, but there was another big war with the SMM crew and the crew of jack boys.

A few weeks ago, Detective Valentines' fellow partner was gunned down during a big shootout at a City Island restaurant. She had been looking at the case closely lately, but the video was all so blurry she couldn't make out what took place.

Besides work, she had been focused on her love life with Knight. She planned to move in with him soon. They had plans to go out of town on a ski trip next week, and she couldn't wait to spend some time with him.

Never had a man treated her so well, so she had been lost in the rapture of love. She pulled up to the witness' apartment and prepared to hear what she had to say.

Detective Valentines had heard it all in her days as a cop, so nothing shocked her.

***

### Uptown Bronx

Lil' K had to go pick up Red from the nail salon on Gun Hill Road. He had plans to take her out for dinner and treat her like the queen she was.

Today was Red's birthday, so Lil' K wanted shit to be on point for her. Lil' K booked a private jet to fly out to Vegas for the night to give her a night to remember.

He saw a small stand with teddy bears, flowers, and traffic candy on sale, so he pulled over.

"Can get some pink roses and a teddy bear?" Lil' K asked the African man selling everything.

Big Blazer drove through the Uptown section of the Bronx to meet with one of his clients. When he saw Lil' K on the corner buying roses, he pulled over in the middle of the street in broad daylight. Big Blazer wasted no time jumping out and letting his .45 spit.

*Bloc...*
*Bloc...*
*Bloc...*
*Bloc...*

Lil' K watched bullets hit the African's chest and spun around with his gun out, firing back at the big nigga in the middle of the street.

*BOOM!*
*BOOM!*
*BOOM!*
*BOOM!*

Big Blazer took cover behind his car and watched out for the bullets as people watched the gunfire from a distance.

When Lil' K saw Big Blazer pull off, he did the same.

\*\*\*

Gun Hill Road, Bronx

Red and Chanel B walked out the nail salon, waiting on Lil' K. They had been kicking it a lot lately, like sisters.

"How are our birthdays two days apart?" Chanel B said.

"Facts, that's why we gotta turn up." Red started dancing in public as men eyed her sexy.

A blue G wagon with tints pulled up. Both women hopped inside Lil' K's truck while Chris Brown and Young Thug's song "Go Crazy" blasted on the radio.

"What's up, babe?" Red said, kissing his cheek.

"Your girl coming with us?" Lil' K pulled out the shopping center lot.

"Where are we going?" Red didn't know where they were going.

"Private jet to Las Vegas, ma." Both women got hype.

"I'm down," Chanel replied.

"We're out," Red said.

They took the private jet to Las Vegas and had a blast, drinking and vibing.

***

Las Vegas, Nevada

The first night in Vegas, Red treated Lil' K to a threesome in the master bedroom, which had a jacuzzi area and beautiful view.

Red and Chanel B fucked and sucked Lil' K to sleep.

"Damn, girl, you need to show me that trick how you spin on that dick," Chanel B said, walking downstairs with Red.

"You gotta teach me that deep throating trick. That shit be hard for me to get it all the way down," Red admitted.

"You have to relax your throat muscles." Chanel B had been sucking dicks in her early teens, so she had that shit down pat.

"That was fun, but I can't front, you ate my pussy like Lil' K on a Henny night," Red laughed.

"I told you I'll rock your world," Chanel B bragged.

"Facts, but thanks for coming," Red stated.

"Look, I'm not a fake bitch, and I'll fuck with you, but I know who you are, Red. I know you really want Money, and I hate him, but I think I'm falling for you." Chanel B saw that look on her face.

Red couldn't believe Chanel B had been hip to her this whole time. She didn't even know what to say.

"I hope they don't come between us, but I've been trying to kill Money, but it's hard to get at him," Red admitted.

"Well, if it counts, I'm all for you and Lil' K. I hate my baby father, so whatever you are trying to do, I'm down.

"Let me go holla at Lil' K real quick." Red got up, and Chanel B slid her finger into her wet slick, making her moan.

Chanel B then licked the cream off of her finger sexually.

"You so freaky." Red walked off.

Red woke Lil' K and told him everything. Lil' K called Chanel B upstairs and asked her if she wanted to be down with his crew, and she got gas.

They had another three-way love session again. Red told him, "Don't get used to this."

# Chapter 25

Harlem, New York

The Kingdom Park basketball tournament this year took place in a YMCA gym.

The place was overloaded with people out to watch the latest moves and best dunkers in the city. Kazzy and Lil' K came out to get out of the Bronx for a second. Lil' K told his brother about the crazy threesome he had in Vegas.

"I can't believe how grimy these bitches is, real facts," Kazzy stated over the loud music and loud crowd.

"Facts, son, but…" Lil' K paused when he saw Big Blazer, Holiday, and a crew of thugs walking in the gym like they owned it.

"But because it's litty." Kazzy had two ski masks in his back pocket and pulled both out and gave Lil' K one, who didn't say a word.

The next couple of seconds happened so fast, nobody saw it coming.

At first, Holiday thought he was bugging when he saw two gunmen running across the basketball court with ski masks on. When he saw a Big Blazer pull out and go to work, he knew it was litty then.

*BLOC…*
*BLOC…*
*BLOC…*
*BLOC…*

Big Blazer fired at the gunmen and ended up hitting a basketball player as a whole place went up in chaos. Everybody ran around in circles, dodging bullets and screaming for their lives.

Lil' K sprayed round after round into the crowd, hitting four teens and a kid in a wheelchair.

*BLOC...*

*BLOC...*

*BLOC...*

*BLOC...*

Lil' K and Kazzy took the side door to the main street with a group of people. Once in Kazzy's car, it was bumper-to-bumper cars racing outside, but Kazzy managed to get away from the police.

"Fuck!" Lil' K banged the dashboard. Kazzy knew why Lil' K was upset. He'd just killed a handful of kids.

"It's good, bro, chill out. Shit happens, just be easy." Kazzy hopped on the highway and lit a blunt he had in the arm rest.

Kazzy knew killing innocent people was a part of the game with living with the thought of the price one had to pay.

\*\*\*

Denver, Colorado

Detective Valentines got out of the shower to prepare for her and Knight's evening together. Knight had gone out to buy her some gifts, so she had enough time to get loosened up and put on something sexy.

They spent the weekend in a large cabin on a small mountain full of snow and slopes.

The ski slopes were so fine, she couldn't get enough of it, while Knight really feared for his life on the slopes.

Opening the top dresser for her panties, she opened the wrong one and saw an outfit that looked familiar. Within seconds, it hit her that the outfit she saw was the same outfit the gunman had on who was in the City Island shootout with her ex-partner, who lost his life while off duty.

Her mind raced so fast she got dizzy.

Downstairs, she heard someone come inside.

"Babe," Knight yelled, making her close the dresser drawer.

"Yes, babe, I'm getting dressed." She rushed to get dressed, hoping her mind was playing tricks on her.

Romell Tukes

# Chapter 26

Elmsford, New York

Kobe drove all the way to Elmsford every morning for work as a truck driver.

His brother, Head, didn't want to take the good route and become a legit business owner like him. Kobe owned a trucking company with three 18-wheelers, which his employees used to drive around the country to do work with big companies.

With a big family of four, Kobe had no time for playing around in the streets risking his life.

Climbing out his car after he parked in front of his place of work, a car was waiting and a Spanish man got out, approaching him at 8:30 a.m.

Kobe hated the morning time, but he knew in his line of work, he had to be at all times friendly.

"Good morning, sir," the man said, standing on the curb.

"How can I help you?" Kobe asked, checking out the man's attire.

"You're Kobe, the owner of Kobe Trucking?" the man asked with a folder in hands.

"Yes."

"I saw your information in the yellow books and I'm looking for a job. I have my CDL and three 18 wheelers up and running in Greensburg."

"Okay, come in. It's the perfect time because at the moment, I'm looking for new drivers." Kobe led the man inside, hoping he found a new driver, because one of his drivers was fucking up, coming in late and always drunk.

When Kobe heard a familiar click, he stopped and turned around to see a gun pointing at his head, almost making him shit on himself.

"Sorry, playboy," Paco told him.

*BLOC...*

*BLOC...*

*BLOC...*

*BLOC...*

Kobe's body hit the floor, and Paco smoothly left the workplace as fast as he came inside.

Paco had been on Head's line for a week now, trying to kill him, but he always got away. So, keeping an eye on Kobe was the next best thing.

While driving back to the Bronx, there was a black Acura in his rearview mirror that seemed out of place. Paco knew he had to test the waters, so he picked up the speed on the Benz and saw the car behind him do the same.

There was a Taco Bell fast-food restaurant on his right, so he made a quick right, trying to shake the car in traffic by pulling into the parking lot.

"Let's play, nigga." Paco parked and jumped out with a 50-cal handgun and rushed the car.

When he saw the person's eyes widen behind the wheel, he tucked his gun just in case someone saw him.

"Yo, what the fuck are you doing here?" Paco shouted at Avona and said it all.

"Huh... I-I-I thought you had another bitch, Paco. I've been calling you for a while. I didn't know what to do," she cried.

Paco saw tears roll down her face and red flags went up. The bitch was crazy.

"I never told you we were a couple," Paco told her to clear up any misunderstanding.

"We had sex, Paco. What the fuck you mean? I'm not just some thot you can fuck and throw away," she yelled.

"Avona, you tripping. Holler at me when you calm down and are able to talk." Paco turned to walk off, and the unthinkable happened.

Avona struck him with her car before racing off the lot. Two older women saw the event unfold and rushed to Paco's aid to help him.

"Sir, do you need medical attention?" one of the women asked, trying to help Paco up, who broke his ankle and knee cap from the hit.

Paco couldn't believe what Avona did. This was why he hated dealing with crazy, bugged out bitches.

"I'm okay." Paco sat up slowly, almost falling over again.

"You need help, sir."

"No, I'm okay, just help me to that Benz," he asked both of them, taking them by the shoulders.

Paco had a gun on him, so if they called the police, it would be all bad, and going to jail today wasn't in his plans, especially after killing someone.

Seconds later, police cars flew by 10 cars deep, going toward Kobe's job.

Paco drove off in pain, getting on the closest highway, thinking about how he planned to kill Avona when he saw her again.

117

Romell Tukes

# Chapter 27

Miami, Florida

Knight got off the private jet from New York to pay Stephen-Stephen a visit.

Today, StephenStephen was throwing a big party at a club for her birthday.

He stepped off the plane wearing an all-white outfit, looking like money. StephenStephen waited for him, leaning against an all-red Rolls Royce Wraith, looking sexy in a mini Chanel dress with a little dab of makeup.

"Happy Birthday." Knight approached her, giving her a hug. She smelled so good he wanted to hug her again.

"Thanks."

"Where are we going?" Knight asked, opening the door for her.

"You taking me out, nigga. What the fuck you mean? First, we got to change you out of that outfit." She looked at him while dashing out the lot.

"Girl, this shit Louis Vuitton." Knight shook his head, because he was a Bronx nigga, so getting fly was all he knew.

"Sorry, boo boo, but we don't do no Louis down here in the 305," she boasted, turning up Lil' TJ's album.

"What do you know about Lil' TJ?" he asked.

"I like him. Oh, I forgot he's from the Bronx." She drove to Collins Avenue to take him shopping real quick at a designer outlet.

"How's business?" Knight asked.

"Same day, same ole." She kept her eyes on the road while talking.

Business for her had been booming the last couple of months, because she'd been dealing with some Texas and New Orleans niggas.

Stephen opened a shop in Houston and New Orleans to sell her product.

"Good."

"What's popping with you, big dawg? I've been hearing a lot about you." Stephen admired Knight's hustle and grind.

"Shit litty, ma, but a nigga got so much I don't even know what's what up there. Niggas dying left and right, I'm just trying to stay focused," Knight told her, as she parked, and then they walked across the street together.

"I'm here if you need me, Knight," she said, walking into the Dior clothing store.

StephenStephen's birthday party weekend was turned up for three days in a row. Knight didn't get a second of sleep. They partied night to day. She even brought a gang of bitches to her mansion to have fun.

Knight could have fucked StephenStephen and a mob of bitches, but he didn't. Instead, he just laid back, enjoying her birthday weekend.

\*\*\*

Brooklyn, New York

Chanel B picked up her son from daycare, and now she was on her way home. Her son's snores made her laugh because when he woke up, he turned into a little monster.

Red text her earlier asking her if she had plans for next week, because she and Lil' K wanted her to come out to California with them to go to Compton.

When she pulled up to her apartment, Money stood in front of her apartment building. She hated Money because of the simple fact that he was a deadbeat.

"What do you want, Money?" Chanel B got her son out the car.

"I want to see my son, bitch," Money told her, blowing smoke in her and the baby's face.

"He's sleep, and I'd appreciate it if you don't blow smoke in our faces or call me a bitch, you deadbeat." She made him laugh with her comment.

"I ain't come to argue, ma. I'll be back." Money walked down the block.

Chanel B walked up the stairs, upset. Money just blew her vibe. The nigga ain't do shit for his son, so she had no respect for him.

Money got to the end of the block and saw Bugatti Boy rushing toward him from across the street.

*BLOC...*
*BLOC...*
*BLOC...*
*BLOC...*

Money used a mailbox as his shield while firing back at Bugatti Boy, who stood on the curb letting his gun bark.

*BOC...*
*BOC...*
*BOC...*
*BOC...*

Money saw his wild shots hit Bugatti in his chest, making him stumble backwards.

Bugatti fired a couple more rounds before he saw Money leaving. Chanel B pulled up and threw Bugatti in the backseat and took his gun while taking him to the hospital.

Chanel B saved his life. He was forever grateful, and her beauty struck him. She stayed with him the whole night. When the police came, they said nothing to the pigs.

# Chapter 28

Soundview, BX

Holiday waited for his grandmother to come out of her two-story house he recently bought her, down the street from the projects he grew up in.

The city was brutal up where violence turned the city into a warzone, and Holiday had been moving differently, unlike Big Blazer. His boy had been moving through with 20 shooters and all types of weapons, trying to catch the opps.

Tonight, Holiday's people were throwing a big party in Club Exit 11 in New Jersey. Money was already out there now with some bitches waiting on him. Head was also out there ready for the party.

Holiday's grandma was on her way to night church for Bible study, and she took her religion seriously. She dressed like an old lady with a long dress, blazer, and a big hat to match her own fly.

When she opened his car door and placed her purse in the seat, the unthinkable took place.

*Tat...*

*Tat...*

*Tat...*

*Tat...*

Bullets ripped through her upper frame as her body slammed into the door panel. Holiday ducked before pulling off. He could have been next.

*Tat...*

*Tat...*

*Tat...*

The two shooters ran across the street, jumping in the fast car, dashing down the block.

Kazzy and Bugatti Boy thought they had Holiday, but his grandma was good enough.

They knew about the big party in Exit 11 in New Jersey since the whole town talked about it. Rappers, actors, and pro athletes would be attending the event, so that meant a lot of police would be there, so Kazzy wasn't up for it.

Lil' K and Red thought differently. They were tailing Head and his crew out there.

"How does a son leave his grandma for dead, fam?" Bugatti Boy asked, driving back uptown.

"When bullets start flying, that be a nigga's first reaction to get away from them hot slugs, feel me, my G." Kazzy looked at the dirty city he loved to death out the window of the Hellcat.

"I hear that." Bugatti Boy had other shit on his mind at the moment.

\*\*\*

New Jersey
Hours later

That night, Club Exit 11 had the biggest party of the year and Head enjoyed it. He made a change in his plans but had stepped out the club with two bitches on his way to an after-party in Newark. One of the bitches Head had with him was on her way to the after-party, so he planned to follow them.

Head got in his truck, following the two women's Benz to the highway. The D'ussé he was drinking had him feeling nice as he listened to a Fivio Foreign's new mixtape. As the music boomed in his ear, he stopped at a red light.

Before the light turned green, a Porsche truck pulled up on the side of him.

*Boc...*

*Boc...*

*Boc...*
*Boc...*
*Boc...*

Head got shot in the arm before pulling off into the street-light, smashing his car hood into the windshield.

Lil' K and Red drove off, hoping he was dead, before hitting the freeway back to New York through the tunnel connecting New Jersey and New York.

\*\*\*

Bronx, New York

Detective Valentines drove to a local diner to meet with Knight, who she hadn't spoken to in a week. When she got back from her trip with him, the only thing on her mind was the outfit she saw him with.

The outfit Knight had was the same the man wore the night her partner got killed in a shootout in City Island. What made everything come to light after looking at the footage she could barely see, was the necklace the man had on.

The necklace worn in the shooting is the same chain Knight wore almost every time she saw him. The footage she had couldn't be used in the courts at trial because the shooter's face couldn't be seen due to the blurry video. Tonight, she had to bring it to the table with her secret she'd been holding onto that she was a cop.

Knight saw Valentines walk inside the diner and stood up to hug her, feeling her vibe was a little off. He hadn't heard from her in a week, and he couldn't front like she hadn't been on his mind heavy.

"Hey, what's the vibe?" Knight asked, taking a seat.

"You." She placed a picture in front of him from the night he killed her partner.

Knight looked at the photo, and he remembered it like the back of his hand, but he couldn't figure out why she had it.

"Where'd you get this?" he asked.

"I'm a cop, a detective. Why were you there?" She had her cop face on now.

"I knew you was a cop from the first time I laid eyes on you, Detective Valentines, and I'm sure you know I'm Knight." When she heard the name Knight, her heart dropped and her panties got wet at the same time.

"You fucking played me." She got upset.

"You played yourself. I really love you, but I live a different lifestyle, so I'm socially distant because I can't be of no help," Knight told her before getting up to leave. Her face said it all. She ain't no if she was coming or going.

# Chapter 29

## Williamsbridge, Bronx

Bugatti Boy pulled into the apartment building underground garage area to where he lived now.

He left Red and Lil' K, who were drinking, smoking, and turning up at the party and having a good time.

Bugatti Boy's life wasn't based around partying but more so getting money and making sure his dad did the right thing and kept his word.

All he wanted to do was get some rest tonight. He had a couple of chicks texting his phone, trying to chill. Parking his big-body Benz, he reached for his duffel bag full of money to put in his safe.

Bugatti Boy had been hustling in Harlem on the Eastside in Carver projects with his boy Nate. One thing Bugatti knew was how to network and get to a bag. No matter what he had to sell, he was going to get money off of it, it just so happened drugs were his place of business.

Stepping out the car, he dropped his iPhone on the floor and picked it up. When he rose up, he heard a soft female voice.

"Turn around in a slow motion," a woman said in a strong accent.

The accent was African. He already got familiar with it during his short stay over there.

Bugatti Boy turned around, looking at an MP5 assault rifle and a beautiful dark-skinned woman behind it, dressed in all black, like she came to kill.

"You going to stare me down or do what you came to do?" He showed no signs of remorse or fear, which made her hesitate.

"I came to kill you."

"I see that."

"But I'm not." She put the gun down and turned to leave.

Bugatti Boy saw how fat her ass was and couldn't let her get away that fast, and not to mention the fact he just had a big ass weapon to his face.

"Wait…"

"What?" she said in her soft tone.

"Who sent you?" Bugatti Boy looked into her eyes. It didn't hit him why she looked so familiar.

"I can't disclose that, but just know you're in danger," she replied before walking off.

Bugatti Boy remembered seeing her on his father's compound, but what did this mean?

***

Mott Haven, Bronx

Kazzy loved getting up early to paper chase, unlike Knight and Lil' K, who both were late sleepers. Since taking over YG projects, he felt like he grew up there.

"What's up, Crip?" a young man said, walking out the front of building 109 with a book bag full of money for him.

Browny had Mott Haven's drug loop unlocked, and Kazzy provided him with the best product in the city at this time.

"Ain't shit, fam, everything correct?"

Kazzy felt how light the bag was, feeling something wasn't right before he opened it. Once he saw the money wasn't real, he looked at Browny who looked back at him, like he just got caught doing something bad.

"Browny, you know it's too early for this shit," Kazzy said before he slapped the fire out of his face before a lot of bikes pulled up.

When Browny's mouth opened to plead, the nigga on the bike sprayed rounds from its submachine gun.

*Tat...*

*Tat...*

*Tat...*

*Tat...*

Kazzy pushed Browny in front of him to block the bullets before he let off shots from his nine millimeter.

Boc...

Boc...

Boc...

Money fled out on the block out the projects, laughing like a mad man on demon time.

Kazzy left the book bag next to Browny's dead body and got the fuck from out of there, seeing people peek out the building windows at him.

\*\*\*

Brooklyn, New York

Hours later, Kazzy went out to have a drink at a lounge by himself to get a clear head, because he felt like he had so much shit on his mind lately.

Everywhere you went in the Bronx, it was like a scene from the movie *Final Destination*.

A cute little chick approached him and just started talking for close to an hour. By the end of the night, Kazzy and the woman were in her bed fucking like animals in the wilderness.

Romell Tukes

# Chapter 30

Bronx, New York

Detective Valentines rode back to the precinct building after meeting in Manhattan with the chief of police and other powerful people.

"Good morning, Detective," a cop said, getting on the elevator with her.

"It's the afternoon call, cut me a break," she shot back, knowing he joked a lot.

"Shit, you work so hard I don't know if you even know what day it is today." The cop made everybody in the elevator laugh.

"Whatever, comedian" she got off on for a walk into her office.

When she stepped foot in her office, she had her favorite type of roses all over the place. She couldn't help but smile until she saw who they came from.

*Detective Valentines, it's always love on my side. I will always be your knight in shining armor.*

Valentines quickly ripped up the note, and she knew Knight was crazy now. A cop, a beautiful white woman, knocked on the door.

"Spill the beans, who's the secret admirer?" the woman asked, catching Det. Valentines off guard.

"Huh?"

"If you can huh, you can hear."

"He's just an old college friend who just got back in town on business." Valentines said the first thing that came to her mind.

"I don't believe that one bit, but I have to play the field, so I'll be back later." She walked out, leaving her alone.

Detective Valentines sat down, thinking what the fuck she would do with all the flowers. She wanted to go call Knight so bad, but she couldn't until she figured some shit out.

Knight's name had recently been brought up by many street rats in connection with over a dozen murders. That last encounter didn't go as she'd planned, but she knew Knight wouldn't be down with helping her, and she respected his code, but she also had a code she lived by.

\*\*\*

Uptown Bronx

Paco hated to text and drive, so he pulled the sports car over into a White Castle parking lot and told D'Aray to get dressed in something sexy for dinner downtown.

He had been cautious lately driving around, not only for the Big Blazer's crew, but he had been keeping an eye out for Avona. If Paco would have had any type of clue Avona was the crazy type, he would have never fucked her.

D'Aray made Paco crawl backwards to her because of her personality and sex game.

Head and two of his girls walked out of the White Castle fast-food spot with bags of food, on their way back to Soundview. The night Head got shot up in New Jersey, the females he left the club with heard the gunshots and the car accident, and spun the block to help Head.

Luckily, the woman was able to get him out the car and to a hospital in time to save his life.

Looking at the white sports car with the blue and yellow license plate that read P A C O, his blood boiled.

"That's an op." Head pulled out his gun at the same time as his crew did.

*BLOC...*

*BLOC...*
*BLOC...*
*BLOC...*

They lit the car Paco was in up so bad, smoke started from the door where all the bullet holes entered, hitting Paco up. Head saw how Paco looked up on a steering wheel and made his getaway with his crew before police arrived.

Two employees from inside the fast-food restaurant called the police. Within minutes, Paco was taken out his car onto the stretcher, and he was rushed to a nearby hospital.

He had a 50/50 chance of making it alive as the EMT workers pumped his chest, giving him oxygen and trying to save his life.

Romell Tukes

# Chapter 31

Bronx, New York

Detective Valentines worked a double today and she was ready to go home and hit her queen-size bed.

Walking at the police station with a double bag, she couldn't believe who she saw standing there leaning on her car.

"Knight, you can't do this," she told him, looking at him as if he'd lost his mind.

"That's what we on, ma?"

"What are you talking about?" She saw police walking past them, giving her and Knight a head nod.

"I'm talking about you not even contacting me. I know we live two different lifestyles, but what about all the love we share? Are you going to throw all of that out the window?" Knight questioned her.

"Knight, you're a gangster, I'm a cop. This ain't that type of vibe. You read too many hood books. This can never be a gangster-type novel lifestyle." She tried to hold back her tears.

"Why can't it?"

"Because this is real life, and in real life, the bad guy can never win," she stated before walking to her driver door.

"Do you still love me?" Knight had to know, and seeing her stop and look at him said it all.

Knight watched her get in the car and pull off. He looked to his left and saw a cop sitting in his car staring at him. Knight smiled and walked off.

\*\*\*

Saint Barnabas Hospital, Bronx

Paco was in the hospital bed, scrolling through his phone and looking at all the missed calls he had.

Getting shot twice was the most painful thing he'd ever felt in his life. He couldn't believe he got caught lacking in a White Castle parking lot, because he hated White Castle food.

Paco barely remembered what happened last night. All he remembered was gunfire then passing out in the car.

The painkillers had him out, but the police left a business card on the table next to him. He didn't see cuffs attached to him in the bed, so he figured the police didn't find the Draco and his stash spot under his backseat.

"You have a visitor." A nurse cracked the door, peeking her head inside the room, then she opened the door all the way.

D'Aray walked inside the room in the Chanel outfit with double the C logo imprinted everywhere.

"Oh my god. I've been here all night," D'Aray said, sitting at the end of the bed.

"How did you know I was here?" Paco gave her a funny look, thinking she set him up, because he knew how bitches were.

"A girl in my building told me she saw your car get hit up. She works at White Castle," she said, telling the truth.

"Yeah, I'm fine." Paco tried to move, but it was hard.

D'Aray tried to fix his pillow, seeing he looked uncomfortable

"I got you," D'Aray said, helping him out, feeling sad for him.

"How long have you been here?"

"All night, I even missed work this morning for you," D'Aray explained.

"I'm sorry, but I got you. How much money did you miss?"

"That's nothing, I'd rather be here with you." She blushed, holding his warm hand.

"I got three thousand in my pocket for you," he told her, seeing her face turn upside down.

"I don't want your money. I know how to get my own bag," she shot back.

"I know, ma."

"Your friend stopped by. I don't know how he knew you were here, but he was out there with me for a few hours until he left," she told him.

"What's the boy's name?"

"Damn, I forgot babe." She tried to think back. "He had, like, a diamond grill with long, neat dreads," D'Aray said, describing the handsome man who called Paco his brother.

"Knight," said Paco, already knowing his boy had his location on his phone like these GPS trackers.

"YEAH, that's his name," she boasted, remembering that had to be the man's name. "He said when you get out of here to call him, but got a question." She didn't know how to ask him this, but if she planned to be with him any type of way, then she needed answers.

"What's up?"

"What are you really into?"

"I live a bad life, D'Aray, and if you're not down, then the door is right there, ma." Paco's tone was cold.

"I'm staying, I just want you to always be honest with me." She looked him in his eyes.

"Always, you know the vibes." Paco and D'Aray chilled until he was able to leave hours later. D'Aray had his car already from the impound lot, so he was happy about that as he took her home, feeling like the king of the Bronx.

Romell Tukes

# Chapter 32

### 187th Street, Bronx

Knight got his dreads retwisted at one of the best salons in town.

He couldn't stop thinking about Valentines and what was going on in his life at the moment. Things in the city had been chilling out for the past couple of weeks as winter time started up.

Khalid kept his word and supplied the best product he ever had since he started selling drugs. Knight truly did miss the days of jacking, but he felt like he was boss'n up now.

"Thank you." Knight paid his hairstylist.

"I'll see you next week," the dark-skinned woman said, counting the $400 he gave her, tipping her nicely.

"Facts, you know the vibes." Knight left the hair salon and saw an NBA player he'd seen on ESPN many times, with the biggest diamond chain he ever saw. Knight followed the man into a dark alley where the man went into the cut to take a piss from all the water he drank today.

"Let me get this, big man." Knight snuck up behind him and pressed his gun to the back of his head.

Knight slid the chain off his neck with his free hand.

"Take it, please bro, you can have the watch too," the NBA player told him with a worried voice.

Knight was more than happy to take the Rolex watch he didn't even know the man had.

"Thanks." Knight walked up the alley, putting on the necklace and watch, feeling like his old self again.

\*\*\*

### College Ave, Bronx

Days later

Big Blazer and Baggs rolled through the city, talking and making plans to go out of town soon on money moves down south.

"How much a key go for down there?" Baggs asked Big Blazer on their way to pick up Big Blazer's little cousin from high school.

"Forty apiece in North Carolina, son, big facts. I need you or Head to slide down there and hold it down. Them Bama ass niggas out there fucked up my bread, boy." Big Blazer pulled up to the intersection of the high school and saw Bugatti Boy walking with a young girl.

"Who down there?"

"Hell nah, we about to pull up on this nigga." Big Blazer grabbed his gun from under his seat, pulling into the high school lot. Baggs ain't know what was going on, but he followed his big homie's lead.

Bugatti Boy had to pick up his little cousin, Trish, from her high school to take her shopping because she just got accepted into a college down south.

"I'm so proud of you," Bugatti Boy said, walking to his car.

When he peeped the Cadillac pulling up, Big Blazer and Baggs hopped out, firing into the crowd of students.

*BOC*...

*BOC*...

*BOC*...

*BOC*...

A bullet hit Trish in the heart and took her out as Bugatti bussed back with a 30-shot clip in his Glock 17.

*BOC*...

*BOC*...

*BOC...*
*BOC...*

One of the shots almost took Baggs' head off as he dropped to the floor and started crawling to avoid getting hit.

Big Blazer saw how hard Bugatti Boy was coming and knew he had to get the fuck out of here.

"Let's roll," Big Blazer said, firing four more rounds, hitting high schoolers trying to get away from the gunfire, but they ended up dying in the midst.

The Cadillac raced out the lot. Big Blazer even forgot about his little cousin he came to pick up.

*** 

Uptown Bronx
Hours later

Lil' K and Bugatti Boy sat in Bugatti Boy's crib after watching Fox News telling the story about the high school shootout that left students dead.

"It's gon' be alright, bro, that's a fact. There will be consequences to their actions," Lil' K said seeing Bugatti Boy's face, which looked soulless, making Lil' K commiserate with him.

"She almost made it to college, bro. What if I didn't pick her up from school? She'd still be alive," Bugatti Boy stated, seeing Baggs' face all over the news for the shooting and wanted for questioning.

"I'ma get up with you, Kazzy, and Paco in Harlem. Hit my line if you need anything, son. Don't stress that shit, fam." Lil' K patted his boy on the back before walking out the spotless two-bedroom apartment.

Romell Tukes

# Chapter 33

## Canaan USP Prison, PA

D Fatal Brim walked out the visit room, smiling after a good visit with a beautiful woman he met on a dating site for prisoners called Write a Prisoner.

Inmates always got on dating sites to catch women, because most prisoners were lonely and doing their time alone. Even though D Fatal Brim had a lot of money, he still was lonely.

Finding someone to do a life bid with them was hard. Some prisoners used females to do time with them financially, but some really wanted love.

The woman D Fatal Brim found was sexy, smart, independent, funny, loyal, and about her business.

Walking back to his unit, he planned to call Knight to see what he'd been up to. D Fatal Brim didn't call people all day every day like other prisoners, who ran their family and friends off by calling them every day.

\*\*\*

## Elmore Prison, New York

Less listened to a group of inmates engage in a serious rap battle on a yard in the cold.

"Spin that shitt," someone in the crowd yelled as one of the battle rappers spit some heat that had everybody jumping up and down for more.

"I'm a hot boy so I got to keep a tool, for niggaz like that 6ix9ine nigga who told on his whole crew," one of the rappers spit, hearing the uproar.

Less' attention was so caught up in the rap battle he didn't see a nigga lurking behind him.

"Yo, mack 050," a friend of Less' yelled, seeing what was about to go down.

At the speed of light, Less turned around to see a nigga who they called Tex swing a razorblade at his face, but he backpedaled and ducked. The scene caught everybody's attention. Even the rappers stopped to watch the show.

Less hit Tex with a mean uppercut and a right hook, knocking him clean out.

"Try again, nigga," Less shouted to nobody in particular before spitting on Tex's face while he laid there sleep like a baby.

Less knew Tex was a SMM, so he knew Big Blazer must have sent him, because Tex was his soldier. With only a couple of months left to the door, Less didn't want to cut him, so he walked off.

***

Bronx, New York

Baggs pulled into the gas station in a rental Jeep with tints, on his way out of town because his face had been all over the news since the high school shooting two weeks ago.

Even though they claimed to only want to question him, he knew better being a street nigger.

Baggs disliked having to kill kids and teenagers, so that day, he felt like shit. He wanted to leave the gang life alone, so he called his cousin in Texas so he could start fresh down there.

Parking next to pump six, he grabbed his wallet, putting on his snapback hat before turning off his truck.

Before he could even open his driver door, seven police cars, all undercover, surrounded him ,blocking him and snatching him out the car, slamming him on the snow.

"You wanna kill kids," one of the arresting officers shot at him before taking him off.

"If it's not SMM Baggs," Detective Valentines cheered, coming inside the single cell bullpen wearing a sweat suit.

"What?" Baggs' mood was fuck the world.

"We saw you on the camera in that high school parking lot, doing your thing. Shit, you should have gone to the Marines," she said, looking at his file.

"Fuck you, I didn't kill nobody," Baggs shouted, almost in tears.

"You did, and if I was you, I wouldn't go down by myself," Valentines said, seeing he was scared.

"Yeah, we know it wasn't you that killed the four high school kids. We saw your boy, Big Blazer," the other cop stated his first words.

Baggs grew silent for a second until they walked away.

"Hold up, what do I gotta do to get out of this, because I swear on my mama, I ain't killed them kids," Baggs cried.

Detective Valentines and her coworker let Baggs out of the cage to start their real case, because the truth was, they had nothing on Baggs or Big Blazer.

The cameras in the school parking lot had been broken for months. All they had was two witnesses who knew Baggs from Soundview projects, but they really wanted Big Blazer and Holiday.

Romell Tukes

# Chapter 34

### Crescent Ave, BX

"Pull over, son, I gotta hit this ATM, you heard," Lil' K told Paco when he came to realize he had no money on him, just credit cards.

Lil' K and Red got into a big fight over some dumb shit, but he knew she got cranky when on her period. When she started throwing dishes at him and shit, that's when he knew he had to get out the house for a second.

He called Paco to come and get him so they could have a boys night out. Club Lust in Brooklyn was having a big party and both men were fly, ready to party and throw some bills.

"Broke ass nigga, you ain't got no cash on you?" Paco asked, pulling over at the ATM on the corner.

Even after being shot, Paco still played the streets, looking for his ops.

"Nigga, spin the block one time. I'll be one second." Lil' K hopped out on a dark block, rushing to the ATM machine.

Lil' K placed his credit card in the machine, taking out a couple of racks to throw in the strip club.

A gray Yukon truck pulled up with tints, and by the time Lil' K looked back, Holiday and Baggs started busting off shots.

*Boc...*

*Boc...*

*Boc...*

"Shit." Lil' K took off to the side of the corner store, getting his gun out. Lil' K pepped around the corner and let off a couple of his own shots as they grew closer.

*Boom...*

*Boom...*

*Boom...*
*Boom...*
When he saw Paco's HD headlights creeping behind the shooters, he fired off more shots, running across the street, dumping.
*Boom...*
*Boom...*
*Boom...*
*Boom...*
Holiday and Head saw Paco jump out busting his Draco as both men started climbing back into the truck pulling off.

"What, were you daydreaming, fam?" Paco joked when they got back in the car. Lil' K wasn't in the mood for jokes today, and it had been a long day.

"Nigga, just go to the club," Lil' K said.

"Yes, sir." Paco turned up the Ace Boogie with da hoodie song "Bleed," driving to the place he planned to never leave until someone buried him.

\*\*\*

### River Ave, Bronx

Detective Valentines drove her work hard through the Bronx, about to take her break. Tonight she worked a double. The graveyard shift sucked 'cause all she got mainly was niggas beating up on a bitches or fiends sneaking in people's homes, with them still in it, to get high.

She was driving back to her office to eat her dinner she prepared earlier at home. Stopping at a four-way, her radio went off, reporting a break-in at a local supermarket.

A car pulled up on the side of her and opened fire.
*Bloc...*
*Bloc...*

*Bloc...*
*Bloc...*
*Bloc...*

Three bullets hit her vest as the rest entered the dashboard before the car pulled off. She made out the shooter's face because he wore no mask. It was Big Blazer who fired the shots.

Detective Valentino called the shooting in on her walkie-talkie, giving the description of the car and reading off the license plate she caught.

Romell Tukes

# Chapter 35

Brooklyn, New York

Chanel B watched her son closely as he played with his father in the park.

This was the first time Money even spent over ten minutes with his son, so she was a little overwhelmed.

She sat on the bench, wondering where did she and Money go wrong, because they had a good bond before she got pregnant. When she was dancing at Albany, he couldn't get enough of her. Now, she felt like she was just a baby mother.

Money and her son started walking towards her, when she peeped the crew of niggas dressed in all black with weapons pop out the bathroom area.

"David!!!" Chanel B yelled her son's name, jumping up.

Money saw the shooters and reacted a second too late.

Boom…

Boom…

Boom…

Boom…

Money's son caught three hits that killed him instantly.

Chanel B got on her knees, crying and screaming, seeing her baby lay dead on the park playground.

*BOC…*

*BOC…*

*BOC…*

Money grabbed Chanel B off the floor, trying to save her life as she tried to fight him to save her dead baby. Gunshots continued to escalate while Money speed off with Chanel B, leaving his son in a pool of blood.

Knight, Lil' K, and Kazzy got inside the stolen van, pulling off, shying away from the crime scene.

"You gotta get the aim together, fam," Kazzy joked with his little brother, who just looked at him.

Lil' K wasn't in the mood to go on hits today, but when he heard Chanel B set up her baby's father, telling Red he was going to be at a park in Brooklyn, he knew it was now or never.

"We almost had that bitch nigga," Knight stated, driving the van back to Brooklyn to burn the car.

\*\*\*

Midtown New York

Knight was out picking up a few items, mainly jewelry for his collection he'd been starting to stack up on over the past few months.

At a hot dog stand, he saw a thick woman with an ass so nice and perfect he could not just walk past. Plus, he needed to get his mind off of Detective Valentines, because she was heavy on his mind.

Last week, he saw her on the news. There was a shooting in the Bronx where someone shot a cop. Hearing her name, chills went down his back, but when he heard she got hit in the vest, he was happy.

Never in a million years did he think he would be cheering for the good guys, especially a cop, but Valentines was honestly someone he held dear to his heart.

"Excuse me." Knight tapped the woman on her shoulder.

"Hey…" She turned around to see the man she knew as Kirk.

"Mita," Knight stated, shocked to see her looking so good.

Knight and Mita had history. When he did his prison sentence in Virginia, she came down there to see him daily while she attended college down there.

"It's so nice to see you," Mita said, giving him a real hug.

"You look great. What you been up to?" he asked, seeing her pay for hotdogs and drinks.

"I'm one of the top DAs in the city, and the youngest, so I've been working hard."

"I see."

"How have you been doing?" She looked at his designer clothes and big-face watch, knowing he was still in the street life.

"I'm trying to open a few small businesses," he told her, walking with her up the block.

"Well, that's great." She really had faith in Knight that he could turn his life around.

"Where you headed to now?" He knew she was in a rush, so he didn't want to really hold her up.

"Back to work. I'm odee busy right now with a shitload of cases ,but take my card and call me." She handed him a business card.

"Okay, I got you. Be safe, sexy," he told her, seeing her blush.

"You stay out of trouble," Mita said before hugging him, walking into her place of work in a tall glass building.

Romell Tukes

# Chapter 36

### Soundview Projects, Bronx

Baggs was released from the precinct weeks ago and since then, he had been working for them people.

On his way upstairs, he had to figure out a way to get Big Blazer to admit to a confession. Setting up his boy had to be the craziest thing he'd ever done in his life. Turning rat was something he never saw himself doing.

He wore a wire in his chain with a small camera recording everything. Walking inside the apartment, he saw four of his homies standing around with guns.

"What's poppin', boy, where Big Blazer at?" Baggs asked as they pointed to the back room.

Baggs went to the last room, down the long dirty hallway, and saw a nice, thick Spanish bitch with curly hair getting dressed.

Big Blazer laid in bed, smoking a big blunt of kush.

"What's poppin', brotty. What's the vibes?" Big Blazer had never been so happy to see his boy.

The two hadn't seen each other since the high school shooting, because they knew being seen together wasn't a good idea. Big Blazer knew the NYPD and gang unit wanted him badly for years.

"Ain't shit, Blazer, I'm just cruising, pulling up to see what's poppin'," Baggs said.

"I thought you went out of town for a while." Big Blazer saw his little bitch he fucked on a monthly basis leave the room.

"I came back yesterday, fam, I miss home."

"Oh, yeah. I heard you was at Exxon station a few nights ago, Uptown near White Plains Road." Big Blazer checked his phone.

"Huh?"

"The bro X said he saw you," Big Blazer repeated if Baggs was good, because he had a worried look on his face.

"I got back the other day or some shit. I've been having so much shit on my mind, I be dead-ass forgetting shit," said Baggs.

"I be knowing, blood." Big Blazer knew killing those teenagers played in Baggs' mind, because it still played in his mind daily.

"I can't believe you killed them kids. I haven't slept since," Baggs stated as Big Blazer looked at him like he didn't know what he was talking about.

"What you talking about, bro?" Big Blazer said, now fully dressed, ready to hit up the after-hour spot in Queens.

"That day I killed those young boys."

"Go home, get some sleep, fam. I'll call you in the morning, and nice chain," Big Blazer said before leaving him in the room.

Baggs knew something wasn't right, but he had to stay focused, because going to jail wasn't in his future.

*** 

176th St., Bronx

Head got off the train at 11:15 p.m., coming from Newburgh, New York, where he had family at. He had his hoodie on as he walked to the top of the stairs, hoping his Uber was already upstairs.

He knew 176th Street belong to the op, so he wanted to be in and out. That's why he called the Uber an hour ago to take him to Soundview.

Head called Holiday, but he didn't pick up, which he did all the time.

A gray BMW with tints waited for him as he jumped in the back seat and saw a white woman driving. The woman looked sexy, but the car was kind of dark inside, so Head stared out the window.

"Soundview Projects, please. You can just drop me off in the back," he told the woman as she pulled off.

"Okay." The woman's voice was sweet and mellow.

When Head realized the woman made a detour down Southboard Way, he thought she got lost.

"You have to go toward West Farms, ma," Head said from the backseat, watching her drive up a path leading into the woods.

"I'm going to turn around," she said, stopping, and then the car doors flew open and two men snatched Head out the back seat.

Kazzy and Lil' K pistol whipped Head for five minutes straight, until their arms got numb.

Red wore white makeup to disguise herself as a white woman, which worked.

"This nigga almost dead." Kazzy looked at Head's face, which looked like a balloon, agreeing with Lil' K.

*Boc...*

*Boc...*

*Boc...*

*Boc...*

Red shot him in his neck.

"Can we go now, please?" She got back in the BMW, ready to go home because they'd been working on her nerves all day.

# Chapter 37

Soundview Projects, Bronx

Holiday couldn't believe what happened to Head.

Seeing his childhood friend on the news ain't sit well with him. He knew who did it and wanted blood for blood.

Tonight, his project was holding a big tribute to Head, giving him a small memorial with candles all over building 77, where he grew up.

The hood had some people in it from all over the city to show respect to the fallen soldier.

"Y'all trying to slide through Michelle Project tonight or Mott Haven?" Holiday asked a group of niggas drinking, in their bag about what happened to bro.

*BLOC...*

*BLOC...*

*BLOC...*

*BLOC...*

*BLOC...*

Hearing the gunfire, everybody took off running, besides the two niggas that got hit. Holiday heard tires peel out. He fired shots at the blue Hellcat racing around the corner.

Two of his men laid in a pool of blood and dirt.

\*\*\*

Washington Heights, New York

Paco cleaned up his crib so D'Aray wouldn't say anything, because she loved to talk shit about how dirty his pad was.

Since getting shot at, he and D'Aray had gotten closer. She was in good company. Normally they would go out and have fun, but tonight she just wanted to chill.

Anytime he would have free time, he would spend it with D'Aray .

Last week he had to change his number, because Avona was blowing his phone up, sending death threats and talking a bunch of dumb shit. Paco wanted to tell D'Aray about Avona, but he didn't want to fuck up something so good.

D'Aray pulled up to Paco's block, looking nice in her hookah dress and heels. Tonight, she planned to rock Paco's world. She wanted him to get her pregnant, so they were going to play pop the condom.

When she got off work hours ago and Paco called her to chill, she was too drained to go out, so she made plans to go to his crib. She hated going over to his spot because it was dirty, but she would help him clean.

Out of the corner of her eye, she saw the same woman who had been following her and Paco for weeks. Enough was enough for her. D'Aray pulled out her 9 mm pistol and approached a white Kia Sedan.

"Bitch, leave us alone." D'Aray's voice scared the shit outta Avona, before shots started to ring out.

*Boc...*

*Boc...*

*Boc...*

*Boc...*

D'Aray ran off down the block in high heels.

Paco heard gunshots outside and looked out his window, seeing a woman in a dress and heels running away from a Kia with bullet holes.

Staring long enough at the woman with the gun in her hand, it finally hit him who she was, D'Aray.

There was no way he was leaving his crib tonight, and now that he knew D'Aray wasn't coming back, he found the porn DVD and jerked off until he fell asleep.

# Chapter 38

Downtown Albany, New York

Aiko lived in the slums of Albany on 4th Street, off of Main Street, where everything happened.

With four kids by different baby daddies, two dead and two locked up serving double-digits, she had to hustle hard to feed her kids and pay bills.

Hustling was in her blood, especially with her brother being one of the biggest dope boys in the city. She and Money got it out the mud. Aiko even had bitches selling pussy to everybody in her hut for her while she waited on the side.

She wasn't the prettiest bitch, but she used to be one of the baddest bitches in the hood until she started having kids every year by local gangsters. Now Aiko weighed over 200 pounds and looked like a hot mess.

Her kids were running around the Section 8 house, yelling and acting a fool, getting on her last nerve.

"Sit the fuck down," she yelled, in the kitchen while making the children dinner.

"Mommy, I'm hungry." Her daughter, who was four years old, was a handful.

"The food will be done in a few, Equiney. Please sit down before I whip your little ass," Aiko shouted, hearing the doorbell ring, stopping her from cooking the children white rice, beef jerky, and green beans.

"I can't get a fucking break, can I," she told herself, wiping her hands to get the door.

Opening the door, she saw a man and a chick standing there.

"How can I help you?" Aiko sold drugs out her crib, but she never saw the two around before, so there was no way she was selling to new faces.

"You Aiko?" the woman asked.

"Yeah, who you?" Aiko thought it was one of her baby daddy's ex or baby mothers. She didn't have time for the games.

Red lifted her gun and fired three bullets in Aiko's face then rushed inside the crib and saw four children. Red and Bugatti Boy looked at each other and knew what they had to do, because the plan was to kill everybody in the house.

*Boc...*

*Boc...*

*Boc...*

*Boc...*

*Boc...*

Seeing the bullets hit the babies did nothing to Red, but Bugatti Boy felt remorse hit his heart as he left the house. Before Lil' K killed Chanel B's son, she told them about Money's sister, Aiko, in Albany, New York, so they waited for the right time.

\*\*\*

Bronx, New York

Detective Valentines hadn't been feeling good lately, so she got a pregnancy test from the CVS store hours ago. When she missed her period, she knew something was wrong, so she wanted to make sure everything was good.

The only person she had sex with was Knight. Valentines washed her hands and looked at the test results, praying it was negative in the CVS restroom.

When the test read positive, she screamed out loud, not out of joy but out of fear and disappointment. At the moment, she didn't know what to do, so she placed the test in her Chanel purse, thinking what to do next. Having a baby with a criminal wasn't in her plans, ever.

Valentines thought she would meet a good, legit man and get married and start a family, but that looked like a dream now.

She had to get back to work, so she put her game face on and tried to block the news out of her head.

\*\*\*

Red Hook, Brooklyn

Fats and Big Blazer sat in the bar having a drink, talking about everything.

"I need a favor," Fats asked while taking a sip of Patrón liquor.

"What's up, fam, anything you need, I am there, bro," Big Blazer stated.

"Do you got people locked up in the state prisons?" Fats asked seriously.

"Of course, my people in every jail."

"How about Elmira?" Fats looked at Big Blazer, hoping he could make his small problem go away.

"Facts, I got a couple of goons up there. What you need?"

"There is a man named OG Bobby up there from Brooklyn. He snitched back in the day and I got 200,000 on his head for whoever comes to end him," Fats stated.

"I got you, big homie, no worry, and this is on the house. I'll hit you when it's done," Big Blazer said as he stood to leave. Big Blazer was locked up with OG Bobby in Attica back in the day, and his name was heavy, so he knew something didn't add up with Fats' story.

Romell Tukes

## Chapter 39

Elmira, New York
Elmira Prison

OG Bobby worked in the prison law library. He was a regular down there.

He spent most of his day off the tier because too much bullshit went on, on his block, being on the tier full of young boys all turned up and trying to make a name for themselves.

OG Bobby helps most prisoners with their cases, so they wouldn't be stuck in here for life like him. With so many years in prison and free time, OG Bobby studied the law in and out.

Tonight, the law library only had six inmates inside, which made it easy on him, because normally, there would be close to 50 niggas yelling and screaming like they had no type of sense.

"Yo, Dead Arm, I'm going to take a piss," OG Bobby told his coworker, who was half asleep in the chair behind the desk.

"Do you," Deadarm shot back before he dozed off back to sleep.

OG Bobby hated working for pennies, but he had very few support out there, mainly his kids and women he met on dating sites.

He went to the stall as he did every time he took a piss to be on point. Closing his eyes for two seconds, he missed the two young blood gang members sneaking into the bathroom.

One of the men stabbed OG in his back with a knife, pushing him into the stall, almost taking him out.

OG Bobby bounced off, catching his balance.

"Come on with that, young punk," OG Bobby said, throwing a combo of punches at one of the attackers, almost lifting him off his feet.

The other man hit OG Bobby in his upper chest twice with the knife.

"Ahhhhhh…" OG shouted before hitting him with a right hook.

The other attacker stabbed OG in his side four times quickly, before seeing OG Bobby slip and fall. Both of the attackers were SMM members under Big Blazer from Soundview projects.

When OG hit the bathroom floor, they were on his line, stabbing him to death, until Deadarm came into the bathroom.

Dead Arm hit one of the attackers so hard he did a backflip, while the other man ran out the bathroom, scared. Deadarm was known for knocking niggas out, and he had a rep to keep.

Looking at OG Bobby slumped on the wall, lifeless in a pool of blood, he knew he was dead.

*** 

Hours Later

Less looked out the bars of his cell with a mirror and saw police packing up all of OG Bobby's shit, who was down the pier.

"Yo, Less," his neighbor said, banging on his wall.

"What's poppin'?" Less responded, trying to figure out what the fuck the guards were doing with OG Bobby's shit.

"You heard what happened, right?"

"Nah, son," Less said, lost in the sauce.

"When I was coming back from the kitchen, I overheard the guards saying two blood niggas ran down on OG in the law library bathroom and killed him," the man stated.

"What?"

"Yeah, boy, that's why we on lockdown, bro, facts," the man said.

"Man, I would have been heard about this, homie, I'm blood," Less said, seeing a guard walking down the tier, shaking his head.

"Yo, CO, what happened to Old Man Bobby?" Less never spoke to the guard before now.

"They told the old man that he ain't stand a chance. I know he was your friend. I'm sorry, man," the CO stated before walking off, smelling K-2 scent in the air.

"I told you," Less' neighbor said.

Less couldn't believe they did that to OG Bobby. He was the most respected man in the prison. That night, Less couldn't even go to sleep after hearing what happened to his old head.

The next day, OG's murder was the talk of the jail, and Less got the word from one of his Hat Boys from the Bronx that niggas were saying Big Blazer had sent the hit.

Less tried to put it together, but it didn't add up why Big Blazer would push the button on OG Bobby.

Romell Tukes

# Chapter 40

Burnside, Bronx

Looking at Avona lying dead in an all-white casket, they didn't know how to react at all.

The funeral service was held outside this nice, windy evening. A lot of people came out to show their support and respect to Avona and her family.

Holiday couldn't believe his sister got killed. She got caught up at the wrong place, wrong time, so the news stated that night her murder was reported.

The killer was still unknown and on the run, but Holiday had a feeling this hit came from his opps. In a few minutes, he had to get up with Big Blazer in Hunts Point.

Holiday told him he wasn't in the mood, but Big Blazer told him it was very important. With everything going on, he would soon need a break from all this street shit.

Unlike Big Blazer, dying in the streets wasn't in Holiday's plans at all. He always had dreams to get out and open up a few restaurants somewhere down south.

Holiday shook hands and hugged friends and family members before leaving the site. He didn't even stay long enough to see his sister's casket dropped in the ground six feet.

\*\*\*

Hunts Point, Bronx

Big Blazer called a meeting with his guys to bring up a couple of big issues. Since Head's death, he had to move different and on point, because he refused to get caught slipping by some goofy niggas who just jumped off the porch.

He parked his car next to the Hudson River, surrounded by warehouses. Holiday's sister got killed, so he knew he had a lot on his plate at the moment, so he planned to cut his boy some slack tonight.

Two luxury cars pulled up, which made Big Blazer smile, because he hated waiting on niggas. The first to hop out was Holiday with an upset face, as if he didn't want to be there.

Baggs got out the Audi truck with a weird look on his face, looking around him, wondering why they came all the way out here.

"Yo, what's poppin', fam? You know today was Avona's funeral, son," Holiday said seriously.

"I know, blood, I send my regards, bro, facts. Avona didn't deserve that," Big Blazer admittedly sadly.

"What's the vibes, bro. I had to go out of town to make some money moves." Baggs was pulling out his chain from under his Louis Vuitton sweater.

"Baggs, I'm glad to see you, but I got a question?" Big Blaser asked, still smiling.

"What's it about, that 200,000 I owe? I'mma have that for you in a few days. It's just the way my bank account is set up, I can only get out a certain amount," Baggs said, making Big Blazer laugh hard as hell, because he remembered that line from a Kevin Hart stand-up show on TV.

"The way your bank account is set up, huh," Big Blazer shot back, seeing Holiday try to read through him to see what he was getting at.

"I got you, though."

"How long have I known you, Baggs, give or take?" Big Blazer asked.

"Twenty-something years, bro. Why you ask?" Baggs had a wry look now.

"I never knew you to wear jewelry, especially some fake shit." Big Blazer walked up to Baggs and snatched the chain off his neck and tossed it in the river.

"Blaze, you tripping, son," Holiday said, seeing him pull out a gun and now aim it at Baggs' head.

"You dirtbag." Big Blazer's eyes were wide and crazy-looking.

"We got history, bro, let's talk about it. I'mma pay you double," Baggs said.

"Nigga, it's not about money, you a fucking rat. You thought I wouldn't find out in my city?" Big Blazer squeezed on the trigger.

"I'm sorry, it's not what you think, son. I swear, the bitch wanted me to get you to tell about the high school shooting," Baggs said, seeing their facial expressions.

Holiday couldn't believe what he just heard.

"Damn, Baggs, how you snuck a nigga like that?" Holiday asked a nigger he called his brother and friend.

"I wasn't trying to go back to jail, bro. You don't know how rough it was for me," Baggs cried.

"Nigga, you out here playing gangsta but you a cold bitch, fam," Big Blazer said his final words.

*Boc...*

*Boc...*

*Boc...*

*Boc...*

Baggs' head taps put him to sleep as Holiday just looked at his dead body, knowing it was time to get out the game.

Romell Tukes

# Chapter 41

Greenburgh, New York
6 months later

Detective Valentines waited outside a shopping center for Knight to show up so she could finally tell him about her pregnancy.

She took off work when she heard her doctor tell her it would be best so she wouldn't risk a miscarriage. Taking off the job she loved was one of the hardest things she ever had to do in life.

In a few weeks, she would be ready to go into labor and bring a little girl into this cold world. Her stomach looked like a basketball as she got in her car when she saw a Bentley pull into the lot.

Seeing Knight get out of the luxury car, she felt old feelings come back. She hadn't seen him in months, so seeing he was still alive and healthy made her smile.

Even though she knew they couldn't ever be together, she still had to accept the fact that he was the father of her unborn seed.

"Hey, Detective." Knight approached her, seeing her large stomach.

"Knight, I'm pregnant with your child." Her words were shocking, but he played it cool.

"Okay, I want to be there to help you, and be a father," he said the right words to make her smile.

"That would be great. I should be going into labor next month on the 16th. I would love for you to come so you can name your daughter," she stated.

"Got you, ma."

"I live out here, so you're welcome to pull up any time, Knight, and stay out of trouble. Your name isn't as hot as it was, so just try to lay low," she said before getting back in her car.

Knight stood there watching her car vanish out the lot, thinking about the news of him about to be a dad.

\*\*\*

Manhattan, New York

Knight took the elevator to Mita's apartment for their dinner date.

The news of him having a seed on the way was the biggest news of the year for him. To be real, Valentines was the last person on his mind, so when she called him out the blue, he knew something had to be seriously wrong.

Things between him and Mita were getting serious, and their chemistry could light up a dark tunnel.

"Hey, handsome," Mita said, opening the door dressed in a nice, classy dress.

"What's up, mami. I see you know how to catch a nigga," he said, walking into the polish apartments.

"I try at times." She blushed, walking to the dining room area where she set up a small candlelight dinner.

Mita couldn't cook, so she ordered food from a local Spanish restaurant she normally ordered from.

"You forgot this," Knight said, picking up a bag full of dessert with receipts stapled to it.

Mita's face looked like she just got caught robbing a bank.

"Oh, that."

"It's cool, you get an A for effort, mami. Plus, I'm starving," Knight told her before sitting down.

"I hope you are really, really hungry tonight," she said.

"I'm always hungry for something sweet," he shot back, catching her off guard, getting her thong soaked between her little cute pussy.

They spent the hour talking and laughing before filling their systems up with liquor, then one thing led to the bedroom.

Mita was on her back with her legs in the air, and screaming his name like she had the Holy Ghost. Knight stroked the soul out of Mita all night long, drunk off the Henny and Moet.

Mita woke up the next morning and Knight was gone like the wind, leaving her confused.

***

Brooklyn, New York

Chanel B had been spending most of her time shopping and getting closer to Money, because he gave her comfort. Tonight, she was going to force herself to tell Money everything about Lil' K and Red.

When they killed her son, that was it for her. She knew she had to draw the line and stay away from them.

Shopping like this was the only stress reliever she had for now. Chanel B left the King Plaza Mall and walked to her car parked in the back.

Two shooters jumped out on her.

*BLOC*
*BLOC*
*BLOC*
*BLOC*

Red saw Chanel B's body spin around and drop on the floor. She was already dead before she hit the floor.

Romell Tukes

# Chapter 42

## Miami, Florida

Fats and two of his goons got off the flight on their way to meet Stephen at some beach with a bar somewhere on South Beach.

Since Fats' old plug, his dad, got killed, he knew he needed to shop for a new connect, and the first name that came to mind was Stephen, the queen-pin of Miami, or at least one of them.

"Boss, that's our limousine in the back," one of his soldiers said, pointing to the last limousine at the end of the line.

"I ain't trying to be down here all day. I don't even know how she look," said Fats, climbing into the limo.

Driving to the location that was texted to him earlier, he hoped he wouldn't have to go elsewhere to find a new plug.

\*\*\*

## South Beach, Florida

Fats told his goons to take a seat on the boardwalk and watch all the bad bitches walk by. He took a seat at a bar next to a beautiful woman, a redbone in a bikini. Fats couldn't help but stare at her body.

"Excuse me, sexy, what's the name of this bar?" Fats thought of anything to ask the woman, just to start up a conversation.

"I believe the name is above your head," she repeated it in a soft voice.

"Oh."

"Where are you from, old head?" the lady asked, seeing the look on his face.

"Old head? Shit, this old nigga will give that pussy a run for your money." He made her crack up laughing, almost falling off the stool.

"You down here to chill or for business?"

"Chilling, waiting on a friend," he repeated, checking his watch, realizing StephenStephen was late.

"How about you telling your goons on the beach we going for a walk." The woman's tone changed.

"I told you, I'm waiting for someone," he replied.

"I know, I'm Stephen, now come on." Stephen grabbed her towel and wrapped it around her waist, covering her fat ass.

"Damn," was all Fats could say, following her down the beach boardwalk.

"So, how can I be any useful help to you, Fats?" she asked, sipping on a fruity liquid drink.

Stephen had 20 shooters all over the place just in case Fats had any ill thoughts.

"I just want to say, it's a pleasure meeting you. They call you the queen of Miami," Fats stroked her ego.

"What do you want? I don't have time for the games."

"I need a new plug."

"What happened to your dad, Rick? Wasn't he supplying New York?" she asked.

"He's dead, that's why I'm down here," Fats replied.

"Damn, I ain't know that Rick was dead. He was an okay dude, sorry to hear that," she said sadly.

"I'm plug shopping."

"I think you may be shopping in the wrong area," she told him.

"My money is good, Stephen. I'm a loyal client, just give me a shot," he started to beg.

"It's not about the money, Fats."

"Then what is it about? Because I'm confused." He didn't understand where she was coming from.

"Do you know Knight?" she said, now stopping.

"Yes."

"Well, he's a close friend of mine, so your money's no good over here. I'mma give you 40 minutes to get the fuck out of my city, that's for you and your men, or you will be leaving in white sheets." She took a sip of her drink and let him know she meant business.

"Okay, I'm going." Fats walked off in a fast-pace, because he heard Stephen was vicious, the bitch got down.

*** 

White Plains Hospital, New York

Knight watched Valentines bring his daughter, Karmela, to the world, and he even dropped a tear of joy. The little girl weighed 7 1/2 lbs and had dimples, good hair, hazel eyes, and nice brown skin.

Knight took pictures and saved them in his phone. He hadn't had a chance to tell Lil' K and Kazzy about the birth of his daughter, but he would soon.

Knight didn't answer the phone the whole night as he spent the night with Valentines in the hospital, talking about future parenting events.

Romell Tukes

# Chapter 43

Uptown, Bronx

Bugatti Boy sat in the clinic, waiting to be seen because some dirty hoodrat burnt him last night.

He couldn't even piss straight. It burned so much he wanted to kill a bitch, but he couldn't even reach her because she gave him the wrong number.

When the nurse came out, she pointed at him, already knowing why he was there from the papers he had to fill out. Over a hundred people came to the clinic every day after being burned by a loved one or a random person they just met.

"Please sit tight in here, sir. The doctor will be with you in a minute, and please don't touch anything." She looked at Bugatti in disgust, shaking her head.

"Bitch," he mumbled as she closed the door behind her.

After he dealt with this, he had to go handle some business with Lil' K because lately, the gunplay over there had been on some Wild Wild West shit almost every night.

They were going back and forth with Big Blazer's crew every night. Last week, a police officer got killed in the crossfire.

Bugatti was playing on his phone when a nigga split in the room with a knife. By the time he lifted his head, Holiday had already pressed his knife in his heart over ten times.

Holiday followed him into the clinic, waiting outside the office until he saw Bugatti walk to the back, and luckily, the fat bitch at the front desk had gone to the bathroom.

Bugatti clutched his heart before falling on the floor, taking his last breath.

As smooth as he came, Holiday left the same way, unnoticed and discreet.

\*\*\*
Miami, Florida
Club G5

Knight didn't have time to be partying in Miami, but Stephen had begged him to come out for her friend's birthday bash.

"How's shit in New York?" Stephen asked over the loud music from Chris Brown.

"Everything is slowly coming back together," he said.

"How about your plug?" She crossed her legs, looking like a boss bitch in her lime green, leather design dress with no panties under it.

"He's doing the right thing, Stephen, but do we have to talk about that? I came to celebrate your birthday, ma," he said, seeing she was tipsy.

"So what do you want to talk about?" She got up and sat in his lap.

The VIP section was private with curtains, so nobody could see them, not even her goons when she was out front.

"Stephen, you drunk," he said as she placed her arms around his neck.

"I'm not drunk, Knight. I just miss you, daddy."

She kissed lips then reached for his belt buckle. A second later, she had her hand around his dick. Stephen started sucking his wood slowly, making love to it.

"Mmmmmmm..." Knight grabbed a handful of her hair and followed her motion, and said he felt himself about to bust.

Stephen got up and straddled herself on his dick and rode his pole until she hit her orgasm.

Knight bent her over on the VIP couch and fucked her all over the area, nutting inside of her.

Stephen and Knight took the party back to her mansion for round two.

\*\*\*

Bronx, New York

Red and Lil' K heard the news about Bugatti Boy's death, and they couldn't believe it.

"This shit crazy," Red said, turning off the TV because the news played the same repeat every hour on the hour.

"What was he doing in the clinic?" Lil' K wondered as Red looked at him in their home.

"Does it matter?"

"Nah, ma, but Kazzy outside. You sure you want to come? This shit may get a little crazy," Lil' K told Red.

Lil' K and Kazzy heard Big Blazer had a basketball tournament in his projects in a few hours.

"Nigga, you know I'm riding," she said, running to the back to grab her Draco and vest.

Romell Tukes

# Chapter 44

Soundview Projects, Bronx

Today was a basketball tournament in the back of Soundview that was turned up to the max. Niggas were doing all types of gravity-defying dunks and jaw-dropping dribbling tricks, hyping up the crowd.

Big Blazer and Holiday threw these types of events to give back to the people and show love to the projects. The night games were also lit in the Bronx.

At the blink of an eye, someone shot out the street lights in the court.

*Tat...*

*Tat...*

*Tat...*

*Tat...*

*Tat...*

People ran around in the pitch-black, getting far away from the gunshots that were coming from everywhere it seemed liked.

*Tat...*

*Tat...*

*Tat...*

*Tat...*

Kazzy put five slugs in the back of Holiday's head before running off to meet up with Red and Lil' K at the meet-up spot.

As Red ran off the court into the crowd, she locked eyes with the one man she was praying to catch.

Before Big Blazer saw the move, he lifted his pistol, but he wasn't fast enough.

*Tat...*

*Tat…*
*Tat…*
*Tat…*

Red hit his upper chest four times before seeing police a few feet away. She took off running to her bike with Lil' K and Kazzy waiting for her on their motorcycles.

The bike dashed through the crowd, making a clean getaway, leaving eight people dead.

\*\*\*

## Richmond, Virginia

Gotti just got a text from Fats talking about Knight, the man he had been hunting for years.

When Knight crossed Gotti and robbed him, he became Gotti's lifetime enemy, and that was one thing nobody wanted on planet Earth. One thing Gotti knew was Knight would pay with his blood for what he did.

\*\*\*

## Brooklyn, New York

D'Aray stayed at her dad's house last night when she had to go to work, so she knocked on his door, seeing that it was slightly open a little.

Stepping into the room, it was dirty inside. She walked over to her dad's office and saw photos. Going through the photos being nosey, she saw a photo of Paco with a target on his forehead.

She almost forgot where she was at. Her hand started shaking uncontrollably as she put the photo down and walked out the room.

D'Aray couldn't let that happen to Paco. She texted him, telling him to meet her in the Bronx. She knew what type of shit her dad was into, and there was no way Paco could be one of the victims.

\*\*\*

Bronx, New York
Hours later

Paco pulled up to the 24-hour food spot to meet D'Aray. It was close to 2 a.m. and he hadn't had much sleep. He couldn't help thinking that D'Aray had been acting a bit distant, but he knew why. Still, he found it almost unbelievable that she had killed Avona. He had thought an op had slumped her.

He saw D'Aray standing on the wall in hoodie, looking like a nigga plotting or something.

"You good, ma?" Paco asked her.

"Shhhh…" She grabbed his arm and brought him into the alley.

"Yo, what's good with you, D'Aray? You starting to freak me the fuck out." Paco pulled her hoodie over her head to see her eyes, if she was high off of some fit.

"They're going to kill you, Paco. We have to leave town," she said, seeing him bust out and laugh.

Paco figured out someone told her about all her people in the streets, but he signed up for death when he signed to the streets.

"It's okay, D'Aray," Paco said.

"No, it's not, my dad got you on his hit list. Everybody he puts on his hit list dies." D'Aray got teary eyed.

"He's gonna have to get in line then, but until then, I'm going home to get some sleep, you coming?" Paco asked.

"Paco, this shit serious. Fats got a lot of people he can send at you, babe, please listen."

Paco heard the name Fats, and it wouldn't leave his head.

"Whose side are you? It's all I want to know, ma."

"Yours," she stated with no hesitation.

"Aight, come on then." Paco got back in his car and she followed him back to his crib to enjoy a night of sex.

\*\*\*

## Harara, Zimbabwe

Khalid raised from his morning prayer in his small mosque. He looked behind him to see his niece standing there.

"How was your trip?"

"Your son is now dead," the woman said, walking inside with her bare feet on the carpeted floor.

"A slow death like I ordered?" Khalid asked, looking at her in her eyes for honesty.

"Yes, Uncle."

"Are you sure?" Khalid picked up two long, sharp darts.

"Yes, I did as you asked." She sensed that Khalid had something up his sleeve.

"You lie to me," Khalid said as he threw one dart into her heart and the other dart in her neck, killing her.

Khalid knew his niece didn't do her job. The way Bugatti Boy died, it wasn't her work. He knew it wasn't her style of training because he trained her himself, and all of his daughters.

\*\*\*

## Elmore Prison, New York

The guards popped Less' cell because he had to go to R&D to go home, finally.

"Yooo, I'm out of here, boy. Shout to all the Macks and Hat Boys on the block. It's too many of y'all to pull up on,"

Less yelled down the tier as niggas banged on the gates, cheering for his freedom.

Niggas loved Less because he'd been putting in work all over, so real Gs respected his handle. Less walked off the tier with property and pictures of his friends at home he looked at every day to get by.

Less got his bus ticket and his $40, plus a credit card with $77,000 on it. Less left the prison in an all-black and white tracksuit, feeling like the king of the Bronx in the middle of nowhere.

***

Bronx Hospital, New York

Big Blazer had been in the hospital for three days since being shot up by Red. The bullets hit his lungs, liver, and his right kidney.

The doctor said he may never be able to walk again, and he was okay with that. The good thing was he made it out alive. Big Blazer could even move his lower body. He knew it could take a long time to heal from this.

Every time he closed his eyes, he couldn't get Red's face out of his head. She was like an unwanted ghost in his dream.

The painkillers they gave him made him sleepy. Big Blazer's eyes slowly closed, and he dozed off in a comfortable hospital bed.

Minutes later, a nurse with a mask came into his room with a food tray, waking him up out of his sleep.

"About time," Big Blazer said, sitting up straight, peeping how the cute little woman still stood in front of him, staring at him.

"Eat up," she said, taking off her mask.

When Big Blazer saw Red's face, he wanted to scream, but he knew this day was coming.

Red pulled out a Glock 40 with a silencer attached to it to muffle the loud noise.

*PSST...*

*PSST...*

*PSST...*

*PSST...*

Red saw blood leaking on the floor from the bed and snuck out the room, closing the door behind her. Red checked every hospital in the city for Big Blazer, and this was the only place that had a patient with his last name.

She took the stairs on her way in and did the same when she exited.

Walking down the stairs, she could have sworn she heard someone but looking behind her, she saw nothing.

When her foot touched the last level of stairs, she saw a man's shadow behind her. Red turned around, pulling out her gun, and saw Money, but her vision was shattered by the sparks of gunfire.

*BLOC...*

*BLOC...*

Two bullets hit Red in her head as the loud noise could be heard throughout half of the building.

Money took off running. He had been trailing her and her crew since the basketball tournament shooting. He attended the game that night, but he was in his car with a bitch getting his dick sucked.

\*\*\*

Across Town, BX
Meanwhile

Knight walked out his crib and saw a letter on his wind-shield. Not too many people know about this hideout apartment, so he got a little worried. He opened the letter and read it out loud to himself.

"Knight, I'm sorry it has to be this way, but this is what is best for us both. I'm moving to the Midwest with our daughter for good. I have a job offer out there, anyway, so it will all work out. I have to play for keeps. I'm sure you can understand that. One day, when the time is right, I will find you so you can build a bond with Karmela."

Knight was speechless because when he was at the hospital, she spoke nothing of this. He crumbled up the letter and got inside his Ford Mustang to meet up with Paco, who said he had some news about Fats to tell him.

\*\*\*

Millbrook Projects, Bronx

Lil' K hung up his phone and ran out of his building where he kept his stash. A nurse just called him from Red's phone, informing him she was shot and in the ICU.

Lil' K ran through the lot and in a swift motion, someone tripped him, making him fall face first on the floor. When the woman took off her mask, he couldn't believe who came to take his life.

Lil' K saw something in her face and eyes. This was the same woman who saved his life before.

"Bahadi," Lil' K said, seeing her lower her weapon before racing off.

Lil' K got up and ran to his car, trying to forget what just took place so he could focus on Red.

\*\*\*

Bronx Hospital

Lil' K double parked out in front of the emergency entrance.

"Sir, you can't," a nurse said as Lil' K flew through the double doors into the hospital, going to the ICU floor.

When the nurse saw Lil' K walking around room-to-room, she stopped him because there were operations going on in another room. It was a busy night.

"Can I help you?" an old nurse asked him with an ID hanging from her shirt.

"My girlfriend was shot," he said, out of breath.

"Sir, five women were shot tonight, but you can't be here."

"Bitch, I'm not going nowhere," Lil' K yelled, causing a scene.

When other doctors and nurses heard that, they all made their way over to Lil' K. The first was a young, fat white lady.

"Sir, what's the problem?"

"My girlfriend was shot and someone called me from her phone."

"I did," a black nurse stated, coming out the room after hearing all the loud commotion.

"Sir, come with me," she told Lil' K, who was now fired up, ready to slap one of the white nurses.

The nurses ice grilled the black nurse, shaking their heads.

"I hate that black bitch," one of the nurses mumbled, seeing Lil' K and the nurse walk off.

"I called you when we found her unconscious body in our stairway. Someone shot her in the head twice," the nurse told him, walking down the shining hall.

"Is she okay?" Lil' K went into panic.

"She's alive. Thank God, we got to her on time," the nurse said sadly.

Lil' K could tell something else was wrong.

"So, she's good?"

"I'll get to that in one second, sir, but first, I believe she has something to do with a patient that died moments before she was shot," the nurse said.

Lil' K did know Red was searching for Big Blazer to make sure he was dead, but he didn't know she made her own plans to come and kill him.

That was something he disliked about Red. The girl didn't listen and was too stubborn.

"I saw her leave the room where the guy was murdered before I went in to check on him. When I saw him dead, I knew what she'd done, but I am from Highbridge Projects. I'm no snitch." The nurse gave him a reassuring look.

"So, this is between us?"

"Facts, but that's not the only issue. The doctor says the cat scan reveals serious damage, and I suspect that there's a better than 75% chance that your girlfriend could lose her memory."

Her words hit Lil' K hard. "So, she won't remember me?"

"It's possible she won't remember anybody, not even her own name," the nurse said, feeling sad for him.

"Fuck."

"She is in room 307. I'll let you get five minutes with her, but she is still in a coma," the nurse said, walking off.

*To Be Continued in...*
Jack Boyz versus Dope Boyz
Coming Soon

# Submission Guideline

Submit the first three chapters of your completed manuscript to ldpsubmissions@gmail.com, subject line: Your book's title. The manuscript must be in a .doc file and sent as an attachment. Document should be in Times New Roman, double spaced and in size 12 font. Also, provide your synopsis and full contact information. If sending multiple submissions, they must each be in a separate email.

Have a story but no way to send it electronically? You can still submit to LDP/Ca$h Presents. Send in the first three chapters, written or typed, of your completed manuscript to:

**LDP: Submissions Dept**
**Po Box 944**
**Stockbridge, Ga 30281**

*DO NOT send original manuscript. Must be a duplicate.*

Provide your synopsis and a cover letter containing your full contact information.

Thanks for considering LDP and Ca$h Presents.

## <u>NEW RELEASES</u>

FRIEND OR FOE 3 by MIMI
A GANGSTA'S KARMA by FLAME
NIGHTMARE ON SILENT AVE by CHRIS
GREEN
THE STREETS MADE ME 3 by LARRY D.
WRIGHT
MOBBED UP 3 by KING RIO
JACK BOYZ N DA BRONX 3 by ROMELL
TUKES

GORILLAZ IN THE BAY V

3X KRAZY III

**De'Kari**

KINGPIN KILLAZ IV

STREET KINGS III

PAID IN BLOOD III

CARTEL KILLAZ IV

DOPE GODS III

**Hood Rich**

SINS OF A HUSTLA II

**ASAD**

RICH $AVAGE II

**By Troublesome**

YAYO V

Bred In The Game 2

**S. Allen**

CREAM III

**By Yolanda Moore**

SON OF A DOPE FIEND III

HEAVEN GOT A GHETTO II

**By Renta**

LOYALTY AIN'T PROMISED III

**By Keith Williams**

I'M NOTHING WITHOUT HIS LOVE II

SINS OF A THUG II

TO THE THUG I LOVED BEFORE II

**By Monet Dragun**

QUIET MONEY IV

EXTENDED CLIP III

THUG LIFE IV

By **Trai'Quan**

THE STREETS MADE ME IV

By **Larry D. Wright**

IF YOU CROSS ME ONCE II

By **Anthony Fields**

THE STREETS WILL NEVER CLOSE II

**By K'ajji**

HARD AND RUTHLESS III

**Von Diesel**

KILLA KOUNTY II

**By Khufu**

MOBBED UP IV

**By King Rio**

MONEY GAME II

**By Smoove Dolla**

A GANGSTA'S KARMA II

**By FLAME**

JACK BOYZ VERSUS DOPE BOYZ

**By Romell Tukes**

## Available Now

RESTRAINING ORDER **I & II**
By **CA$H & Coffee**
LOVE KNOWS NO BOUNDARIES **I II & III**
By **Coffee**
RAISED AS A GOON I, II,  III & IV
BRED BY THE SLUMS I, II, III
BLAST FOR ME I & II
ROTTEN TO THE CORE I II III
A BRONX TALE I, II, III
DUFFLE BAG CARTEL I II III IV V VI
HEARTLESS GOON I II III IV V
A SAVAGE DOPEBOY I II
DRUG LORDS I II III
CUTTHROAT MAFIA I II
KING OF THE TRENCHES
By **Ghost**
LAY IT DOWN **I & II**
LAST OF A DYING BREED I II
BLOOD STAINS OF A SHOTTA I & II III
By **Jamaica**
LOYAL TO THE GAME I II III
LIFE OF SIN I, II III
By **TJ & Jelissa**
BLOODY COMMAS I & II
SKI MASK CARTEL I  II & III

# Romell Tukes

KING OF NEW YORK I II,III IV V

RISE TO POWER I II III

COKE KINGS I II III IV

BORN HEARTLESS I II III IV

KING OF THE TRAP I II

By **T.J. Edwards**

IF LOVING HIM IS WRONG...I & II

LOVE ME EVEN WHEN IT HURTS I II III

By **Jelissa**

WHEN THE STREETS CLAP BACK I & II III

THE HEART OF A SAVAGE I II III

By **Jibril Williams**

A DISTINGUISHED THUG STOLE MY HEART I II & III

LOVE SHOULDN'T HURT I II III IV

RENEGADE BOYS I II III IV

PAID IN KARMA I II III

SAVAGE STORMS I II

AN UNFORESEEN LOVE

By **Meesha**

A GANGSTER'S CODE I &, II III

A GANGSTER'S SYN I II III

THE SAVAGE LIFE I II III

CHAINED TO THE STREETS I II III

BLOOD ON THE MONEY I II III

By **J-Blunt**

PUSH IT TO THE LIMIT

By **Bre' Hayes**

BLOOD OF A BOSS **I, II, III,  IV, V**

SHADOWS OF THE GAME

TRAP BASTARD

By **Askari**

THE STREETS BLEED MURDER **I, II & III**

THE HEART OF A GANGSTA I II& III

By **Jerry Jackson**

CUM FOR ME I II III IV V VI VII

An **LDP Erotica Collaboration**

BRIDE OF A HUSTLA **I  II & II**

THE FETTI GIRLS **I, II& III**

CORRUPTED BY A GANGSTA I, II III, IV

BLINDED BY HIS LOVE

THE PRICE YOU PAY FOR LOVE I, II ,III

DOPE GIRL MAGIC I II III

By **Destiny Skai**

WHEN A GOOD GIRL GOES BAD

By **Adrienne**

THE COST OF LOYALTY I II III

**By Kweli**

A GANGSTER'S REVENGE **I II III & IV**

THE BOSS MAN'S DAUGHTERS I II III IV V

A SAVAGE LOVE  **I & II**

BAE BELONGS TO ME I II

A HUSTLER'S DECEIT I, II, III

WHAT BAD BITCHES DO I, II, III

SOUL OF A MONSTER I II III

KILL ZONE

A DOPE BOY'S QUEEN I II

By **Aryanna**

A KINGPIN'S AMBITON

A KINGPIN'S AMBITION **II**

I MURDER FOR THE DOUGH

By **Ambitious**

TRUE SAVAGE I II III IV V VI VII

DOPE BOY MAGIC I, II, III

MIDNIGHT CARTEL I II III

CITY OF KINGZ I II

NIGHTMARE ON SILENT AVE

By **Chris Green**

A DOPEBOY'S PRAYER

By **Eddie "Wolf" Lee**

THE KING CARTEL **I, II & III**

By **Frank Gresham**

THESE NIGGAS AIN'T LOYAL **I, II & III**

By **Nikki Tee**

GANGSTA SHYT **I II &III**

By **CATO**

THE ULTIMATE BETRAYAL

By **Phoenix**

BOSS'N UP **I , II & III**

By **Royal Nicole**

I LOVE YOU TO DEATH

By **Destiny J**

I RIDE FOR MY HITTA

I STILL RIDE FOR MY HITTA

By **Misty Holt**

LOVE & CHASIN' PAPER

By **Qay Crockett**

TO DIE IN VAIN

SINS OF A HUSTLA

By **ASAD**

BROOKLYN HUSTLAZ

By **Boogsy Morina**

BROOKLYN ON LOCK I & II

By **Sonovia**

GANGSTA CITY

By **Teddy Duke**

A DRUG KING AND HIS DIAMOND I & II III

A DOPEMAN'S RICHES

HER MAN, MINE'S TOO I, II

CASH MONEY HO'S

THE WIFEY I USED TO BE I II

**By Nicole Goosby**

TRAPHOUSE KING **I II & III**

KINGPIN KILLAZ I II III

STREET KINGS I II

PAID IN BLOOD **I II**

CARTEL KILLAZ I II III

DOPE GODS I II

By **Hood Rich**

Romell Tukes

LIPSTICK KILLAH **I, II, III**
CRIME OF PASSION I II & III
FRIEND OR FOE I II III
By **Mimi**
STEADY MOBBN' **I, II, III**
THE STREETS STAINED MY SOUL I II
By **Marcellus Allen**
WHO SHOT YA **I, II, III**
SON OF A DOPE FIEND I II
HEAVEN GOT A GHETTO
**Renta**
GORILLAZ IN THE BAY **I II III IV**
TEARS OF A GANGSTA I II
3X KRAZY I II
**DE'KARI**
TRIGGADALE I II III
**Elijah R. Freeman**
GOD BLESS THE TRAPPERS I, II, III
THESE SCANDALOUS STREETS I, II, III
FEAR MY GANGSTA I, II, III IV, V
THESE STREETS DON'T LOVE NOBODY I, II
BURY ME A G I, II, III, IV, V
A GANGSTA'S EMPIRE I, II, III, IV
THE DOPEMAN'S BODYGAURD I II
THE REALEST KILLAZ I II III
THE LAST OF THE OGS I II III
**Tranay Adams**

THE STREETS ARE CALLING
**Duquie Wilson**
MARRIED TO A BOSS I II III
**By Destiny Skai & Chris Green**
KINGZ OF THE GAME I II III IV V
**Playa Ray**
SLAUGHTER GANG I II III
RUTHLESS HEART I II III
**By Willie Slaughter**
FUK SHYT
**By Blakk Diamond**
DON'T F#CK WITH MY HEART I II
**By Linnea**
ADDICTED TO THE DRAMA I II III
IN THE ARM OF HIS BOSS II
**By Jamila**
YAYO I II III IV
A SHOOTER'S AMBITION I II
BRED IN THE GAME
**By S. Allen**
TRAP GOD I II III
RICH $AVAGE
**By Troublesome**
FOREVER GANGSTA
GLOCKS ON SATIN SHEETS I II
**By Adrian Dulan**
TOE TAGZ I II III

LEVELS TO THIS SHYT I II

**By Ah'Million**

KINGPIN DREAMS  I II III

**By Paper Boi Rari**

CONFESSIONS OF A GANGSTA I II III

**By Nicholas Lock**

I'M NOTHING WITHOUT HIS LOVE

SINS OF A THUG

TO THE THUG I LOVED BEFORE

**By Monet Dragun**

CAUGHT UP IN THE LIFE I II III

**By Robert Baptiste**

NEW TO THE GAME I II III

MONEY, MURDER & MEMORIES I II III

By **Malik D. Rice**

LIFE OF A SAVAGE I II III

A GANGSTA'S QUR'AN I II III

MURDA SEASON I II III

GANGLAND CARTEL I II III

CHI'RAQ GANGSTAS I II III

KILLERS ON ELM STREET I II III

JACK BOYZ N DA BRONX I II III

A DOPEBOY'S DREAM

By **Romell Tukes**

LOYALTY AIN'T PROMISED I II

**By Keith Williams**

QUIET MONEY I II III

THUG LIFE I II III

EXTENDED CLIP I II

By **Trai'Quan**

THE STREETS MADE ME I II III

By **Larry D. Wright**

THE ULTIMATE SACRIFICE I, II, III, IV, V, VI

KHADIFI

IF YOU CROSS ME ONCE

ANGEL I II

IN THE BLINK OF AN EYE

By **Anthony Fields**

THE LIFE OF A HOOD STAR

**By Ca$h & Rashia Wilson**

THE STREETS WILL NEVER CLOSE

**By K'ajji**

CREAM  I II

**By Yolanda Moore**

NIGHTMARES OF A HUSTLA I II III

**By King Dream**

CONCRETE KILLA I II

**By Kingpen**

HARD AND RUTHLESS I II

MOB TOWN 251

**By Von Diesel**

GHOST MOB

**Stilloan Robinson**

MOB TIES I II

**By SayNoMore**

BODYMORE MURDERLAND  I II III

**By Delmont Player**

FOR THE LOVE OF A BOSS

**By C. D. Blue**

MOBBED UP I II III

**By King Rio**

KILLA KOUNTY

**By Khufu**

MONEY GAME

**By Smoove Dolla**

A GANGSTA'S KARMA

**By FLAME**

## BOOKS BY LDP'S CEO, CA$H

TRUST IN NO MAN

TRUST IN NO MAN 2

TRUST IN NO MAN 3

BONDED BY BLOOD

SHORTY GOT A THUG

THUGS CRY

THUGS CRY 2

THUGS CRY 3

TRUST NO BITCH

TRUST NO BITCH 2

TRUST NO BITCH 3

TIL MY CASKET DROPS

RESTRAINING ORDER

RESTRAINING ORDER 2

IN LOVE WITH A CONVICT

LIFE OF A HOOD STAR

Romell Tukes

CPSIA information can be obtained
at www.ICGtesting.com
Printed in the USA
LVHW051757191121
703844LV00017B/1422